MW00831036

ACE

Published by KT Publishing

ISBN: 979-8-9868478-7-0

Cover Designer: Books & Moods

Editing: Victoria at Cruel Ink Editing + Design

Proofreading: Zainab M. at the blue couch edits

To the ones that ignore red flags, justify toxic behavior, and think morally black men are romantic.
Ace is for you.

Warning

If you have any triggers, this is not the book for you.
Your mental health matters.

You've been warned.

Visit www.kylafaye.com for a list of trigger warnings

Playlist

"Enchanted" - Taylor Swift
"Creep" - Radio Head
"Work Song" - Hozier
"Dark Things" - ADONA
"The Night We Met" - Lord Huron
"Jesus Christ" - Brand New
"Power Over Me" - Dermot Kennedy
"The End" - Blue October
"Every Breath You Take" - The Police
"i hope ur miserable until ur dead" - Nessa Barrett
"M.I.N.E (End This Way)" - Five Finger Death Punch

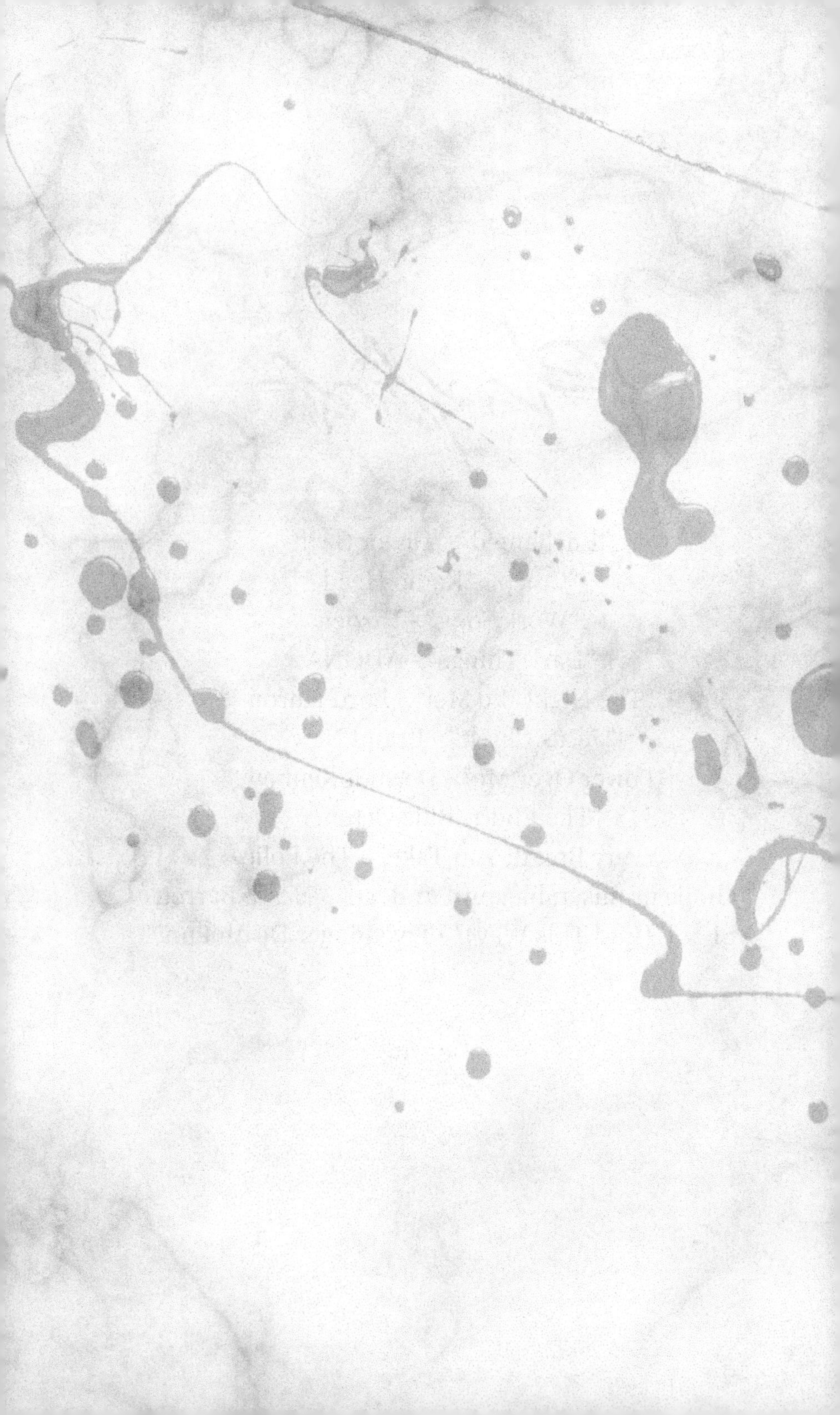

Prologue

Twelve Years Old

I did something bad today.

The worst thing I'd ever done.

I killed Mommy.

I didn't mean to. We were playing. Then all of a sudden, she stumbled over the stupid Nerf gun I left on the stairs and fell...

It happened so fast. Before I could even register what was happening, she landed at the bottom of the stairs, and blood was gushing from her head.

Blood.

So much blood.

More than I'd ever seen before in my young life.

I'd seen blood from nosebleeds, and sometimes, Father made me bleed, but I'd never seen that much before.

It was everywhere, and when I tried to help her, it got on my hands.

My body acted strangely...

The reaction I had, the way everything inside of me sparked to life...

It was unlike any other feeling I'd ever had.

I wasn't exactly sure what that reaction meant, but I instinctively pulled my pajama pants down and used my bloody right hand to stroke the hardening flesh between my legs. I'd seen Father do it before.

He'd always told me that if I wanted to become a man, I had to use it, so I guess that meant I became a man today.

My body had just experienced the best feeling. When Father had come in and seen me standing there above mommy's body, my pants were still down around my ankles, and a pool of white fluid was on her lifeless chest.

"Ace! What the fuck did you do?!" Father yelled, his face turning pale as he took in what happened. I froze at the sight of him. My eyes were wide as I stood before him, holding my breath, afraid to move. Reality hadn't sunk in; I was too high on euphoria to realize the severity of the situation.

"You killed her! You killed your mother!"

He accused me of killing her, and I had, hadn't I? If I hadn't left my toys out, she wouldn't have tripped. Instead of arguing, I remained silent.

"Your mother should've aborted you. I begged her to. I never wanted children, but she did, and I wanted to make her happy." Father looked at me with hatred in his eyes. More hatred than usual.

"You're a bad boy. Get on your knees, and stop fucking crying." I hadn't realized I was fully crying until I tasted the salty tears on my tongue when I licked my lips.

Father gripped my hair painfully, causing me to cry out.

"If you want to be a disgusting boy, I will show you what it's like to be dirty." Father cursed under his breath and forced me to my knees by kicking my legs.

He looked larger than life standing before me, and all I could do was stare at him through my teary, blurred vision.

He removed his pants and forced himself down my throat, and afterward, he held a hand over my mouth. He covered my mouth and pinched my nose, forcing me to swallow the thick, salty fluid he left behind on my tongue. My ears plugged after the first gulp, and I could see Father's lips moving, likely spewing more hate, but I couldn't hear him because of the pressure in my ears that made me feel as if I was underwater.

Bile rose in the back of my throat as I swallowed again, the remainder of the fluid slipping down the back of my throat. I gagged behind his hand, my body shaking, while my mouth filled with vomit, giving me no choice but to swallow down the chunks.

Dark spots lined my vision from the lack of oxygen, and even as I scratched against his hairy thighs, he kept his grip on me.

Finally, Father shoved me away, and I gasped for air, my body shaking uncontrollably as I lay on the floor, curled in the fetal position.

"Clean yourself up. You're disgusting." He spat, and his saliva landed on the arm I held protectively over my face.

I knew my father was evil, but I never knew how much my mother had shielded me from him.

Little did I know, without her, Father was free to act completely unhinged.

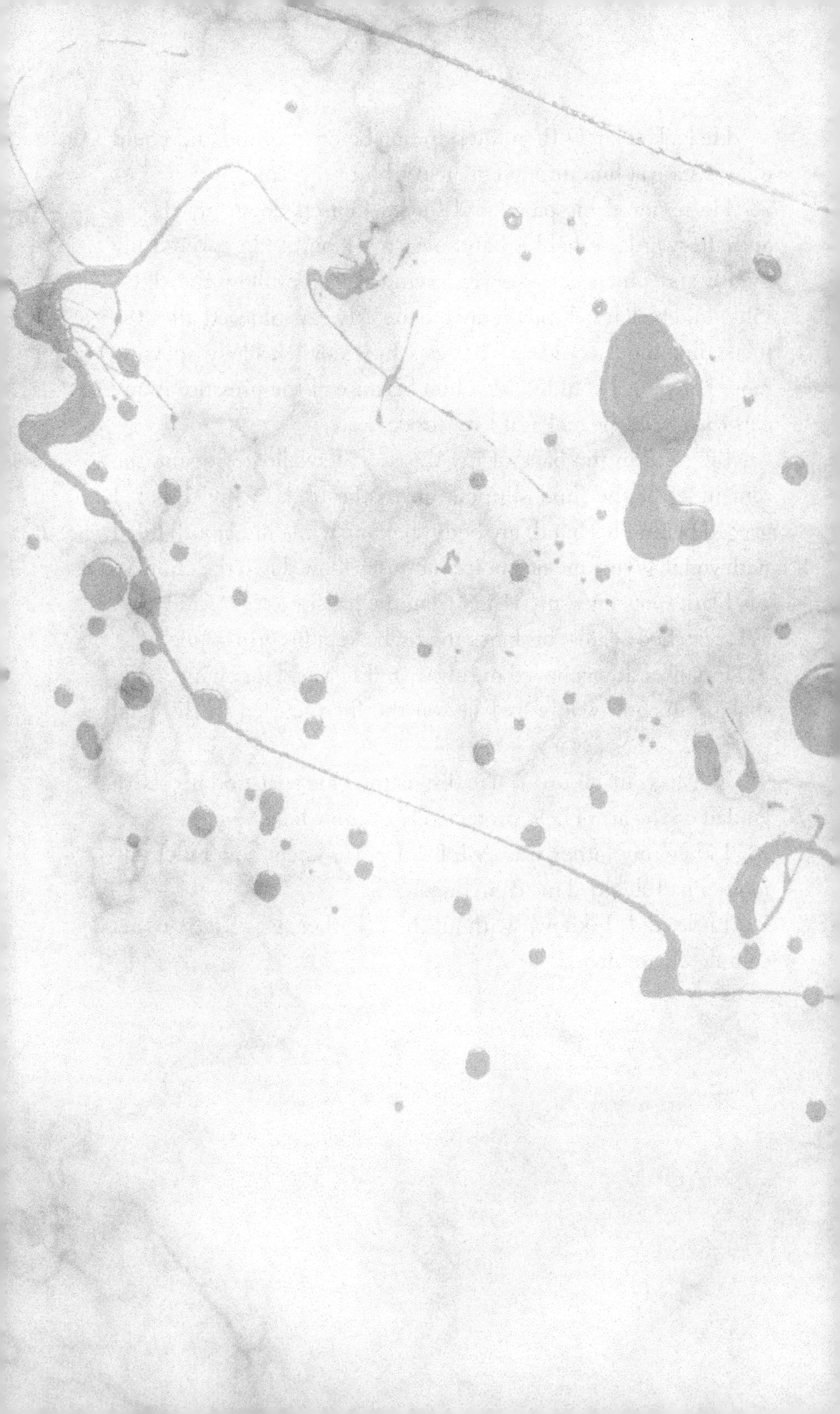

Chapter One

Six months later

Father hates when I come out from the attic, so I rarely do. Usually, I watch from the window until he leaves for work and then come out. Ever since I killed Mommy, he doesn't like to see me anymore.

Father only has time for me when he comes to my room in the middle of the night, smelling of liquor, to punish me.

My punishments started long before Mommy died, but since her death, they've become frequent.

He taught me not to cry, because when I do, he only makes it hurt worse.

We were never a religious family, but after Father would leave my room, I'd pray to God that he'd stop. That he'd realize it's wrong to hurt me. If he stopped, I'd be willing to forgive him.

He's my father, and I love him.

I'll forgive him.

God listened to me, and now, it's been two months since

Father has punished me. It's also been two months since his new family has moved into our home.

Father forgets about me a lot. It's easy to do when I spend my days in the attic, keeping quiet and staying out of everyone's way.

I don't mind staying there. Father's new wife and daughter are horrible. Mommy's been gone for six months, but I'm the only one who misses her.

Sometimes I wonder if I'm the only one who ever loved her.

Father removed all the photos of her we once had on the walls of our home. Every family photo is gone, replaced by photos of his new wife, Sharon.

In a blink of an eye, life as I knew it ended, and the Wicked Witch of the West moved in.

My stomach grumbles as I lie on my mattress on the floor.

Most nights, I'm able to sneak some snacks from the kitchen and hide them away in my room for when I get hungry during the night.

Sharon says I'm too big and should eat less.

She's so dang stupid.

Eating less doesn't stop you from growing. I'm getting taller by the day, and starving me will not stop it. She controls the amount of food I eat ever since I called her daughter fat.

If anyone needs portion control, it's her.

I wasn't being rude when I said it, though. I was being honest. She insulted my appearance by calling me "freakish" because I'm tall and skinny, so I insulted her back by calling her fat and ugly.

It wasn't a lie. Mommy taught me to never lie.

In my defense, she's not ugly because she's fat. She's ugly because of her features. Her eyes are too close together, and one is a little bigger than the other.

Sometimes when I stare at her from across the dinner table, I catch her right eye wandering off while her left eye stares at me.

Her eyebrows are furry, like an old man's eyebrows, and she's always scowling.

She's got buck teeth, her top lip is bigger than the bottom, and her nose resembles a pig. It doesn't help that her name is freaking Penny.

She looks just like her mother, and she's hideous, too. I'm willing to bet if you investigate their family tree, you'd discover more than one cousin fucker.

I know what that is because Father always said Mommy has a weird family line and once called her sister a cousin fucker.

Sharon and Penny are nothing like my beautiful mom.

My stomach rumbles for the fourth time in a row. I have no more snacks up here, and I'm still starving. Once again, I didn't get enough to eat tonight.

Unable to wait until morning, I crawl quietly across the floor until I reach the stairs.

I peek my head down the staircase and listen. I need to get food, but if I run into Father or his wife, they might punish me for being downstairs when I'm not supposed to be.

Last time that happened, Sharon slapped me so hard my cheek stung for hours. Still, I'd prefer her punishments over his—which I thankfully haven't received from him in a while.

Quietly making my way down, I hold my breath as I stand on my tiptoes and tread into the kitchen. I'm just about to make it to the glorious white fridge that's calling my name when I hear a door creak, followed by a whimper.

Penny the Pig has my old bedroom on the main floor. When they moved in, she decided she liked the room and wanted it. Despite there being three empty rooms upstairs, Sharon insisted Father place me in the attic. According to her, my devil eyes scare her, and she doesn't want me sleeping close to her.

The Witch and Father share a bedroom upstairs. It's the bedroom he once shared with my mother. That filthy pig is now sleeping where my mom used to and attempting to fit into her clothes. No matter how much sucking in or Healthy Choice frozen meals she eats, she'll never be as petite as mommy.

Leaning my back against the wall, I place a hand over my mouth to keep myself from letting out any noise, saying a silent prayer to God that no one is awake and coming to discover me out here. I know I'll get in trouble, and my dinner plate is already so small that I can't stand the portions getting any smaller.

Whenever I look at myself in the mirror, I'm able to see my ribs protruding from my skin. No wonder everyone calls me a freak. I am one.

With my shaggy black hair, pale skin, mismatched eyes—thanks to my heterochromia—and being tall while nothing but skin and bones. It's true what everyone says about me. I am a freak.

Whimpers steal my attention away from my inner pity party.

"My sweet Penny. You are such a good girl; do you know that?" I hear my father's voice, which causes the hair on my arms to stand up and a knot to form in my stomach.

Oh no.

I recognize the dark, sultry timber of Father's voice. I've heard it every time he's called me a *bad boy* and punished me.

"Good girls get rewards between their legs. Would you like that, my sweet Penny?" he says, and I'm unable to hear what Penny says in response.

"Good girl. Tonight will feel just as good as all the other nights." *All the other nights?* Realization sets in like a sucker punch to the gut.

Penny is the reason why Father no longer visits my bedroom at night. He's visiting her instead. He's hurting her the same way he hurt me.

Or is he?

Father calls me a bad boy before he holds me down and

punishes me, but Mommy would call me a good boy while she knelt between my legs, delivering pleasure instead of pain.

Is Father rewarding Penny like Mommy did me?

Does he love her the way Mommy loved me?

With my hands balled into fists and shaking at my sides, I sneak closer to the cracked bedroom door and peek in.

The image of my father on top of Penny, his body between her legs, his bare ass flexing as he thrusts into her small body, is enough to make me nauseous.

No, no, no. This doesn't look right.

My nails break skin and dig into my palms.

I probably made a noise, because Father suddenly stops, looks over his shoulder, and his dark eyes stare into mine. I think he's going to stop, but his mouth forms a grin, and he continues thrusting into a whimpering Penny.

"Don't be a freak and stand there watching. Come here, boy. Let me show you how a real man takes care of his woman."

Unable to help myself, I gravitate toward them, ignoring the blood that's dripping down my hands. It's going to be painful to pull my fingernails out of my palms once I unclench my fists. Certainly, I'll have scars from it.

I'm familiar with what Father is doing, but it doesn't feel appropriate to witness it happening to someone else. I learned from watching shows I'm not allowed to watch that it's against the law and morally wrong.

My favorite show is about stuff like this. That pretty lady, detective Olivia Benson, puts people like my father in jail. Does that make Penny and me special victims?

Will Olivia arrest Father? She says this is wrong. She says men who hurt children are bad.

Father is bad.

Finding courage, I speak up, "She's not a woman." I hiss the words with venom on my tongue. "I'm calling Detective Benson."

Something snaps inside of me, and for the first time, this man isn't my father; he's my prey.

With the rustling of sheets and Penny's hissing, my father grabs the back of my hair and pulls me back against his bare, sweaty chest.

"Good luck calling a fictional character, you fucking idiot. That damn mother of yours should've put your stupid ass in school instead of choosing to homeschool you. Maybe if she had, you'd know the difference between reality and a goddamn TV show." Father laughs, his fist tightening in my hair.

It doesn't matter if *Law & Order* and Olivia are fictional. There are real people like her who can help us.

"I'll call the police!" I warn, silently patting myself on the back for having the courage to stand up to my father. Whether I like Penny or not, I'll protect her the way I wish someone would've protected me.

"You are not calling the fucking police, you little freak! If you do, I'll tell them it was you. I'll tell them you killed your mother, assaulted her body, and then fucked your stepsister. Do you think they'll believe you over me?" He laughs into my ear.

Tears sting my eyes, but I force them back. I've gotten pretty good at hiding my tears and pretending not to cry.

Gripping my shoulders, Fathers turns me around to face him, grabs my white T-shirt, and uses it to wipe the blood off his flaccid cock. Disgust fills my stomach at the sight of Penny's blood on my shirt.

I cautiously glance over at her lying on the bed, but instead of finding a scared, crying thirteen-year-old girl, I see her scowling at me like I have taken her favorite toy away.

What did I do wrong?

"Go to bed, Ace. Forget what you saw here. If you speak of this again, you will spend the rest of your life in prison. And in prison, they don't like boys who fuck their stepsisters." He shoves me backward and away from him, and I stumble but quickly catch myself before I fall.

I run toward the stairs that'll lead me to the attic. I don't care how loud my steps are; I need to get back to my safe space.

Once back in my room, I hide under my covers, let my tears fall, and pray that hiding under my blanket will be enough to protect me from the monster lurking below me.

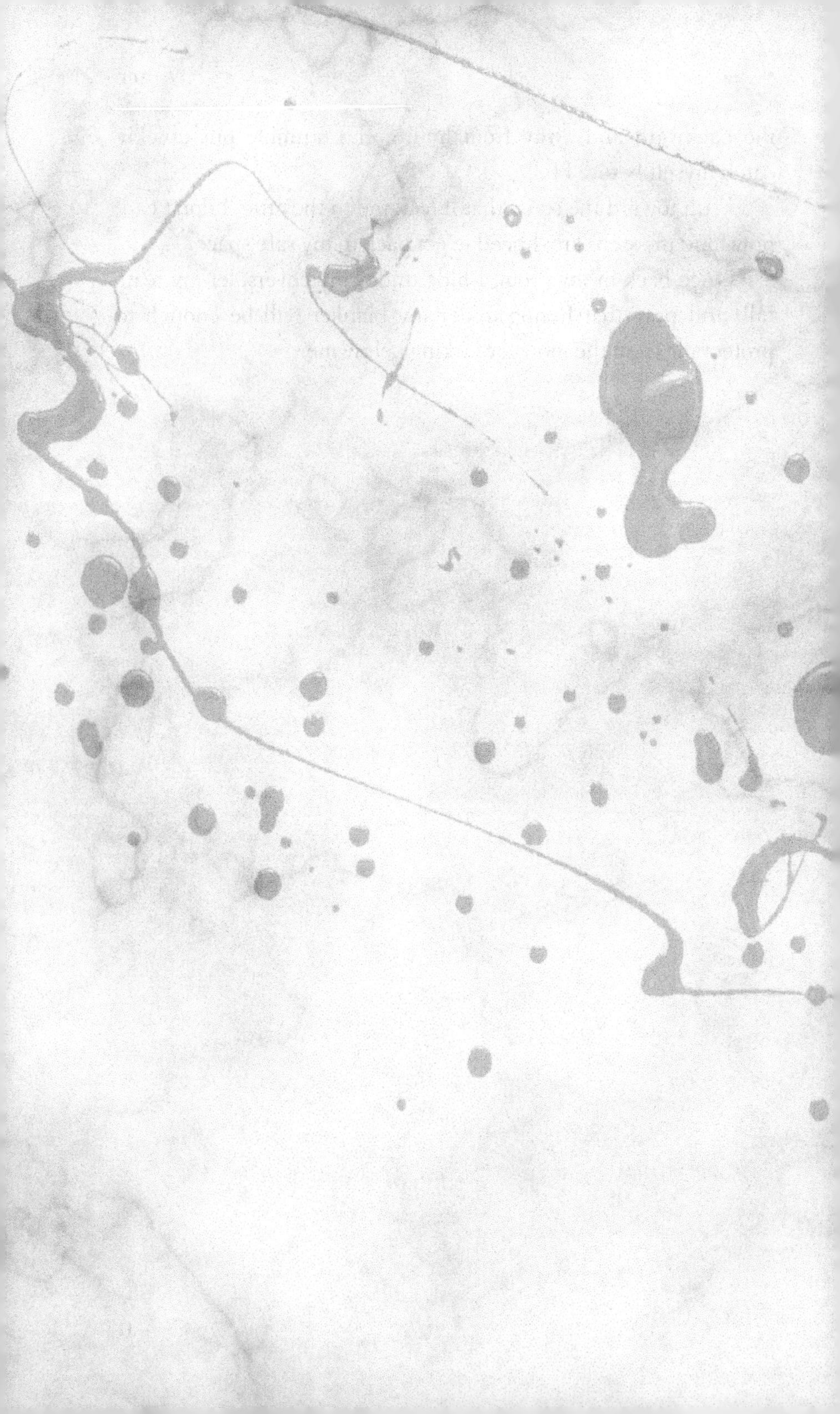

Chapter Two

It's been two days since the night I caught Father hurting Penny.

Two days since I've seen either of them.

I'm so disgusted and unable to face them, so I've been staying in my room until it's time for Father to leave for work, then I sneak downstairs.

Sharon doesn't work and is always home. Since it's summer break and we don't have school, Penny is home, too. Luckily, I haven't run into them, and Father hasn't yelled up the stairs for me to join them for dinner either, like he typically does.

I'd be lying if I said it's been peaceful. It's been anything but, and I've been waiting for the other shoe to drop.

I feel in my gut, just as I always have, that something is about to happen. I felt it the day my mom died too, but I ignored it, choosing to continue playing instead.

This time, I can't ignore it. My hunger and anxiety pushed me to take another risk and go downstairs again.

I'm standing at the fridge, shoving grapes into my mouth,

when I hear Sharon scream. I don't care about her, but if she gets hurt and is screaming for help and I don't help, I'll be the one in trouble. Lately, I've been trying to avoid drawing any further attention to myself.

"Penny!" Sharon screams, and I quickly shove the container of grapes back into the fridge and let the door slam closed as I take off running toward the screaming.

In the laundry room, Sharon is on her knees and in tears in front of Penny. She has something in her hands, but I can't see what.

My eyes widen once I finally see what she's holding.

Small pink cotton underwear with hearts on them, with a blood stain on the crotch.

Oh, God.

My heart races, and my stomach aches as if it's signaling to me that the something bad that I've been fearing is about to happen now.

I can see their lips moving, but the thump of my heart trying to escape from my chest is so loud I have trouble clearly making out what they're saying. The bits and pieces I'm able to understand are only a few words, but enough for me to know this isn't going to be a good situation.

"What happened? Did you get your period?"

"N-n-no. I... was hurt."

Finally, Sharon looks up, her blue eyes filled with rage.

"He did it. He hurt me," Penny says, pointing directly at me.

For a moment, I hope my father has returned home and is standing behind me and that's who she's pointing at, but a quick glance over my shoulder tells me I'm not that lucky.

"You hurt my daughter!" Sharon screams, standing to her feet, charging at me like a bull who has just spotted someone waving a red banner.

"No, no, I didn't! I swear! It wasn't me!" My sight blurs as tears roll down my cheeks, and I hyperventilate. "Please, Penny, tell the truth!"

"I swear it, Momma! He hurt me." Penny bursts into tears, causing Sharon to step away from me and rush to comfort her sobbing daughter.

I should run away. Leave this house and never return, but foolishly, I pray that when Father returns home, he'll protect me from Sharon and get her to calm down and believe that it wasn't me.

In the back of my mind, I know it's wishful thinking, but what can you expect from a twelve-year-old boy?

I'm hoping my father will protect me. But deep down, I know he won't.

I've been sitting in front of the window for hours, waiting for my father to get home, and as soon as he does, I hear doors slamming below me. Then, Sharon screams.

"Your freak of a son raped my sweet little girl! I want him out of this house!" Her voice is like nails on a chalkboard. It hurts my ears, but somehow, my heart hurts even worse.

I never touched Penny, and I never would. I tried to protect her by threatening to call the police, but Father is right. It's his word against mine. Who's going to believe our town's beloved lawyer over a child? A child that everyone already thinks is a freak.

Despite my height being above average for my age, I'm still a child. My mommy isn't here to protect me anymore, and she always did when it came to Father. Whenever I called my mother "Mommy," my father would get upset with me. He'd ask me if I were a baby, and when I'd reply, he'd hit me in the back of the head and tell me only babies say *Mommy*. Then he'd tell me I need to grow the fuck up and start talking like a man.

Sometimes, he'd throw me outside and lock the doors, telling me to go play and make friends so people would stop thinking I was a freak.

Our neighborhood was one where, during the summer months, the adults would get together for barbecues while the other kids played. They'd ride bikes outside, play video games inside, or even toss a ball around in the front yard.

Instead of joining them, I always preferred keeping to myself. Sometimes, I'd climb through the window when Father would lock the door. I would stay inside and work on the computer. Before Mom had me, she worked cybersecurity. She'd told me so many stories about her days in college and the things she did at work. She was brilliant, and often she'd do some freelance work from home to help old friends and colleagues of hers. I think she worked for the government. Her work was always top secret, but the times I peeked, her screens were filled with funny looking codes.

The first time I saw her in action, I knew I wanted to be just like her when I grew up. So, instead of playing, I taught myself how to code. I still have a lot to learn, but one day, I'm going to be just as good as her. I just know it.

Father always laughs at me. He tells me hackers go to prison, and Mom's lucky they didn't lock her up. I'm not sure why she would've been taken away, but regardless, his negative words will never stop me.

"Ace! Get the fuck down here!" Father's booming voice causes me to jump at least three inches off the ground.

Uh-oh. It's time to face him.

My face heats, and goosebumps form on my skin as a chill rushes down my back. I take my time standing from my torn and stained mattress on the floor, stretching out my limbs. I can't wait until I have muscles and I'm not so wimpy-looking. I'm practically Slender Man, that creepy guy from video games.

"Ace! Get out here, now!" Father yells, followed by the inaudible screams from Sharon. It's obvious they're having an argument, but her high-pitched and squeaky voice makes it difficult to understand.

Placing one foot in front of the other, I leave the comfort of my bedroom and make my way into the living room where I hear the raised voices, followed by the sobs of my evil stepsister, who steps behind her mother the moment she sees me. I don't know why she's crying and pretending she fears me. We both know that I've done nothing to her to warrant her fear.

The lump in my throat prevents me from speaking. He knows I didn't hurt Penny, but he won't tell Sharon otherwise, and if I do, they'll all accuse me of lying. Sharon never believes me anyway, and Father hates me for what I did to Mommy.

It's three against one.

As much as I want to believe he will protect me, the knot in the pit of my stomach tells me he's not going to.

"You little piece of shit! I knew you were a bad boy! You have the devil in you, boy," Sharon screeches, turning her meaty body sideways to wrap her arms around her daughter in comfort.

"James, call the police! I can't look at him anymore. Look at what he did to my baby." She steps back, waving her arms in front of a crying, red-faced Penny. She looks fine, other than she's fake crying.

"Enough, dammit. We're not calling the police," Father snaps, his loud voice stern and full of authority.

"Why the hell not?!" Sharon demands. "They should lock him away with other little freaks like him!"

"Ace has brought enough shame on this family. I do not want our name ruined any more than it already is." He taps his chin as if he's deep in thought, his dark eyes staring right at me.

"Well then, what the hell do you plan on doing?"

"He's going to leave this house," Father decides, a grin spreading across his thin lips. "As of this moment, Ace, you are no longer my son, and this is no longer your home. You killed your mother, hurt your sister, and have been a disrespectful little shit toward Sharon. You will not be a part of this family for another day."

My eyes burn with unshed tears at Father's harsh words. "You do not get to speak." He looks toward Sharon and Penny. "I'll be back. Go, take our daughter upstairs."

Penny peeks around her mother's body to look right at me. A slow, devious smile spreads across her face before she leaves the room, disappearing with Sharon.

I turn to Father to plead my case, "Please, Father, please. Don't send me away. You know I didn't hurt her, and I swear I'll tell no one it was you. Ever! Please!" I fall to my knees at his feet, begging.

I'm a kid. I'm *his* kid. How can he do this? He can't send me away, right?

"Get your ass up. You're embarrassing yourself." He scoffs, looking at me in disgust. "I never wanted you. Your mother was the only one who wanted you, and I wanted her to be happy, but you took her from me. Now, you're no longer my problem."

Father always told me that crying was a sign of weakness. I learned a long time ago that crying only provokes him, so I learned to keep my tears to myself. Unfortunately, this time, like many times this week, I fail, and the heavy, endless tears fall from my eyes. Although, I've mastered silent crying. I can cry without movement and without a single sound.

"How can you do this? Please, Father, please."

"It's incredible what can happen when you want something badly enough." He chuckles, bending down until we're nose-to-nose. "Your Aunt Willa helped me with the paperwork a long time ago. I've just been waiting for an excuse to get you the fuck out of here." He keeps his voice low, staring into my teary eyes as he breaks my heart.

"I-I-I'm staying with Aunt Willa?" She's Mommy's sister and has always been nice to me. I'm willing to stay with her until Father loses his temper.

"Fuck no." Father takes away my only hope of being with family, the only person who reminds me of Mommy. "You'll probably go to a foster home. Maybe even a group home, wherever the fuck it is. I don't care." He stands, brushing invisible lint from his clothing.

"Let's go." When I don't move, he grabs a fistful of my hair and pulls me toward him.

I cry out, my scalp burning from the grip he has on my hair. He leaves me no choice but to shuffle after him on my knees as he drags me away from my home.

"Father, please! I'll be good! Please! You can punish me, but let me stay. Please!" I beg, pleading with him, but my sobs fall on deaf ears. He doesn't care, nor does he bother to look at me.

He allows me to stand once we're out the door, and I follow him to his car in defeat.

"Get into the fucking car!" he yells, climbing into the driver's side. Taking one last look over my shoulder, I glance back at the yellow house with the white door that I grew up in. My memories with my mother—my happiest moments—are all here.

Movement in the window catches my eye, and I look up just in time to see Penny standing in the windowsill with a smile on her face. Before I turn around, the little bitch sticks out her tongue, holds up her hand, and flips me the middle finger.

With a scowl, I turn around, climb into Father's car, and dry my tears while he drives me away and into the unknown.

It's okay. He just needs to give Sharon time to calm down.

Everything will be alright, and I'll be back home soon.

He's my father. He has to keep me.

This is only temporary.

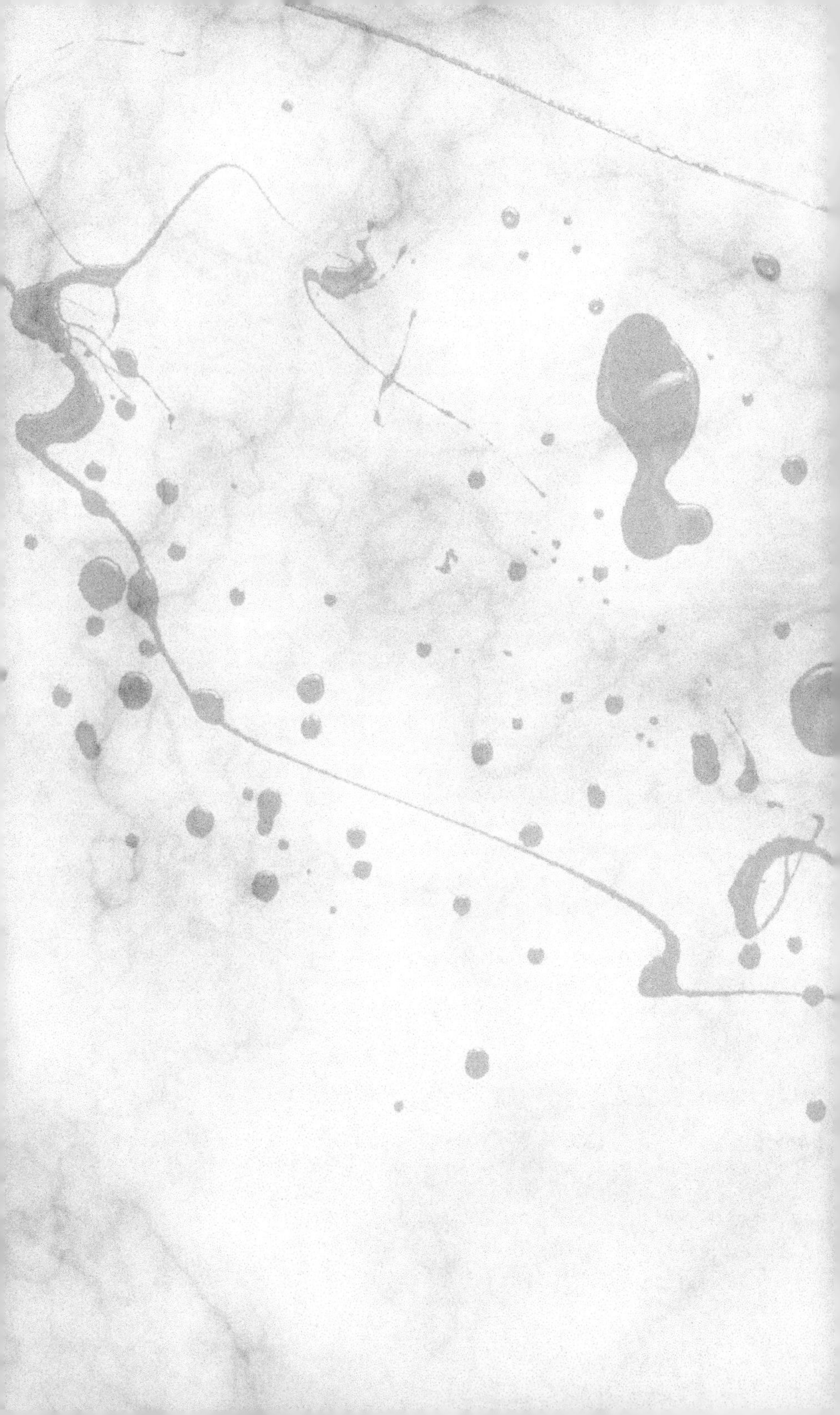

Chapter Three

Three months later

Fuck this place. I hate it here.

Sometimes I wish I were back with Father in the attic on my faded, torn mattress on the floor. At least that was better than sharing a room with four other boys, and only having a sleeping bag and the world's thinnest pillow to sleep on. There are two sets of bunk beds in the room, but they're all claimed already, leaving me to sleep on the floor.

At least the sleeping bag is new, but the pillow is as old as this house. I don't have a pillowcase, so I get to smell the musty stench and see the yellow stains all night. Most nights I don't even use it, but sometimes I tire of using my arms as a pillow. It's not very comfortable.

One day, I'm going to have a gigantic bed with a hundred pillows. I'll sleep like a king and get a solid eight hours every night.

One day.

I'll also have so much food that my fridge overflows, and I'll never have to experience hunger pains again.

One day, I'll have a perfect life.

One day.

At least that's what I tell myself to keep from crying myself to sleep every night.

One day, things will be better. I'll be an adult and can make my own decisions.

Foolishly, I thought Father would return for me, but it's been three months, and according to my caseworker, Stacey, they're looking for permanent placement for me.

The day when father had taken me to Aunt Willa, I was hopeful I'd be able to stay with her. But she said her house was too full at the moment and couldn't take me in. She fed me cookies and milk while she sat with me in the living room, waiting for the caseworker to pick me up and take me to a new home.

When Stacey came, I begged Aunt Willa to keep me, but with tears in her eyes, she turned her back on me, telling me she was sorry.

That's how I ended up here.

Father doesn't want me anymore. I never knew it was possible to give away your twelve-year-old child, but I'm proof that it is.

Noise in the room reminds me I'm not alone and breaks me away from my thoughts.

"Did you see the new girl?" Jesse, my foster brother, asks Clay, who's lying on his bottom bunk, spinning a basketball in his hands.

I listen to their conversation from where I lie on the floor, counting spots on the faded yellow popcorn ceiling.

"What? She's here already? I thought she wasn't coming for

another few days?" Clay responds, the bed squeaking, as he pulls himself to sit on the edge.

"Nope, her caseworker just got here with her. They're in the living room." A few days ago, I overheard that we'd be getting a new addition to this horrible house.

A girl.

She'll be the only girl here, apart from Marla, our foster mother. Knowing my four foster brothers, I feel bad for her, but not too bad because I know she'll be just like them. I already know she'll hate me without even knowing me because everyone here does.

Clay, Chad, Jesse, and Alex have hated me since the day I arrived. Unless they're mocking me, they don't speak to me. I've tried to make friends and make the most of our situation, but they think I'm a freak. Who can blame them?

"Let's go meet our new sis." Clay stands, his attention turning to me. "Hey, freak, are you coming to meet the new girl?"

With a sigh, I sit up on top of my sleeping bag, looking directly at him. I open my mouth to speak, but think better of it, and opt for shaking my head.

"Good idea. Don't want to scare the poor girl her first night here." He laughs. Before I can register what happens next, he raises his hand, throwing his basketball directly at my head. It's not the first time, and I know it won't be the last. The first time he hit me in the face, he gave me a bloody nose. Marla blamed me, and I got the belt that night for staining my shirt with blood.

The ball bounces off my forehead with a thud and lands in my lap. Clay leaves the room, his laughter echoing behind.

He's right, though. I'll likely scare the new girl, and from what I've heard, she's just a kid. Well, I'm a kid, but I don't feel like one. I feel like I've lived a hundred lives already.

I'll stay away from her. It's for the best.

It's nearly ten o'clock by the time Marla calls us all into the kitchen for dinner. My stomach has been growling all day, and as it got later and later, I doubted that we'd get dinner tonight. She forgets to feed us a lot, and on those days we're lucky if we're able to find a cabinet unlocked to sneak a snack.

Marla says she doesn't have enough money to keep five growing boys fed, so she keeps locks on the cabinets and fridge. I'm not sure why she says that though, considering she receives monthly checks for each of us. She doesn't work, unless you consider playing bingo a job and then, in that case, she's employed full-time plus works overtime. She's always away at the bingo hall downtown.

Walking into the kitchen, I stop in my tracks when I see the new kid for the first time. She stands next to Marla at the island, holding a paper plate in her small hands while Marla places two slices of cheese pizza on her plate.

The savory aroma of the pizza fills my nostrils, causing my empty stomach to growl loud enough that it catches her attention.

The girl with the blonde halo of hair looks up, her unreal turquoise eyes staring right at me. I feel shy and feel the need to run and hide again, like I've been doing since she arrived this afternoon.

I've had enough rejection, and I'm one more rejection away from hiding in my sleeping bag and crying. Either that or slitting my wrists like I've seen Jesse do before.

The girl stares at me as I stand there awaiting her judgment, then slowly, so painfully slow, a smile lights up her face, and her eyes brighten.

At that moment, right then and there, I decide that she's mine. She's my new pretty thing, and I want her to look at me like that for the rest of my life.

"Ace! Quit being weird, boy, and come get some pizza before it's all gone," Marla snaps, opening the second box there on the counter. Today must've been a good day at bingo if we're getting pizza. Or she's trying to make a good impression on the new girl. Hopefully, she doesn't get used to it, because tomorrow we'll be back to stale crackers and expired cans of tuna.

Leaving the comfort of the corner, I step further into the kitchen and stand beside the girl, grabbing a paper plate from the stack.

"Freak," Jesse mumbles, not so quietly under his breath, earning a laugh from the rest of my foster brothers.

The blue-eyed girl doesn't laugh. Instead, she offers a smile. "Hi. I'm Lee," she mumbles, keeping her eyes locked on me, looking at me as if I'm going to be the one to save her from this nightmare.

I wish I could, but I'm drowning as much as I know she will be. From things I've overheard about her, I know that this is her first foster home, but it won't be her last. That's something I've come to learn, even though this is my first home. You can never allow yourself to get too comfortable, because there's no such thing as security when you're in the system.

Despite the smiles she's freely giving me, I can tell she's sad. The first night is the hardest. It's been months since my father tore me away from my home, and it's still hard. Every single stupid night here is hard.

There's no hope of being adopted at this age, so you must suck it up and come to terms with the fact you'll be here until the day you age out.

After dinner, I'm placed on kitchen clean up duty along with Chad while Marla takes Lee and her ratty pink backpack into the third bedroom of the small house. I've seen the room and know that it's identical to mine.

That's the girl's room, and the blue-eyed girl will be the only one in there. According to Alex, there were two girls, sisters, living here right before I arrived, but their parents regained custody and they got to go home. There's been no recent additions since me.

Those girls are lucky. Their parents wanted them, could fight to get them back, and proved they were good enough. I think they're stupid for losing their kids in the first place, because how do you lose something that's already yours? It's not like they lost their phone or a pen. They lost their children. Someone went into their home and removed their kids because a court decided they were unfit.

That makes little sense to me.

My mother never would've lost me, and if she were still alive, I'd be at home right now. Safe and in her arms, being loved and wanted. I wouldn't have to be here in this dirty place. But that's my fault because I killed her.

This is my consequence.

This is what happens to bad boys who hurt pretty things.

Once upon a time, I was wanted, but not anymore, and I wish to be wanted again. There's no one to make me feel wanted, and it makes me sad. My heart aches all the time.

Mommy wanted me and loved me. Every time Father left for

work, we had our special time together and she showed me how much she loved me.

Until I ruined it.

When Mommy told me I hurt pretty things, I never thought that was true until that night.

The night that changed the rest of my life. If only I would've listened to her and cleaned up. I wish I had been a good boy for her.

I have many regrets and replay that day in my head, wishing I had done things differently.

Unfortunately, no matter how badly I wish I could change what happened, I can't.

Later that night, under my sleeping bag, listening to the sounds of the four boys around me sleeping, I close my eyes and replay that day.

Except, this time, I don't change the events of what happened. I replay everything. Mostly, I replay Mother's bloody scene and how my body reacted at the sight of the thick crimson pouring out of her open wound.

My body reacts without my consent, and just as I did the first time this happened, I let my urges take control and wrap my hand around the hard length between my legs and stroke until my body shakes, and I release my warmth into my boxers.

I don't get up to clean myself. Instead, I roll over and fall asleep, sleeping the best I have since the day Mommy died.

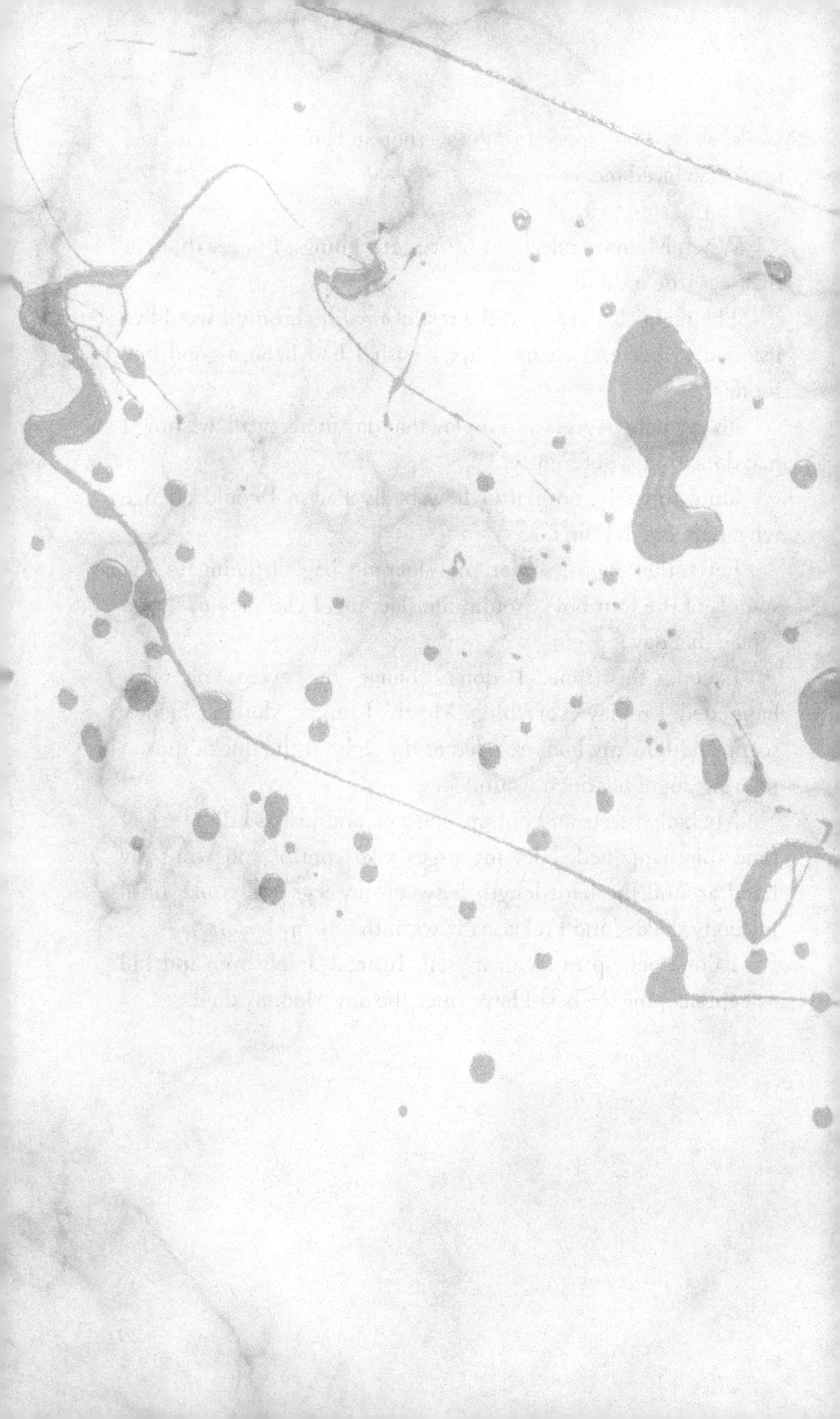

Chapter Four

Two weeks have passed since the arrival of the girl with golden hair and ocean-like eyes. Days after she showed up, two other girls did too, Jessica and Dana.

I had hoped they'd be as nice to me as Lee has been, but they took one look at me lurking in the kitchen corner one day and decided I was weird. It didn't help that Clay was right there to call me a freak in front of them, making them giggle and run off together.

Fuckers.

I hate all of them. Every person in this house, except her. Never her.

How could I ever hate the pretty girl who never stops sharing her smiles with me? She's the only ounce of happiness I have in this place, and I know if I'm not careful, I'll steal that happiness from her.

It's what I do.

I ruin everything.

I break pretty things.

I'm a bad boy. Father told me so on the nights he'd come into my room and shove my face into my mattress, pull my pants down, and hold me down while he hurt me.

Between his grunts, he'd tell me how much he hated me and how bad I was. His words were cruel and hurt worse than what he'd do to me.

Bad boys get punished.

Jesse must be bad too, because this morning when I walked into our bedroom after my shower, I saw Alex behind him on the bottom bunk of the bed giving him a punishment, making the same sounds Father made.

I'd stood there for sixty-eight seconds before they noticed me. I counted in my head, just like I did when Father would deliver my punishment. Every time he entered my room, I'd begin counting, waiting for him to leave.

Alex had noticed me first. "Get the fuck out, you freak!" he yelled at me, his hips still moving behind a moaning and groaning Jesse.

"Fucking freak!" Jesse hissed, throwing a pillow at me before I finally left the room, not bothering to close the door.

If he was getting punished, then everyone should know that he was a bad boy too, and he deserved it.

I'm not the only bad boy around here.

The thought of telling Marla is playing around in my head when laughter suddenly fills the silence. "I bet you're a virgin, huh, freak?" I sit at the kitchen table with a sandwich in my hands, but Alex chuckles and slaps it out of them. To my dismay, the simple ham sandwich falls apart, stale bread landing on the floor.

Instead of responding or paying him any attention, I lean forward, pick up my fallen sandwich from the floor, and put it back to together before I resume eating.

The five second rule doesn't apply when you're around assholes who like to mess with you. Sometimes it takes twenty or more seconds. A little dirt doesn't bother me because I don't waste food. Besides, the floor is clean. I know that because I'm the one that cleaned it this morning after Marla complained about the kitchen being filthy, even though it wasn't because I got stuck with kitchen duty last night.

"He probably doesn't even know about sex," Clay chimes in, slapping down a pornographic magazine in front of me on the table, the page open to reveal a naked woman with the largest breasts I've ever seen and smooth silk between her legs. She looks different from the only naked woman I've ever seen.

He's wrong, but I'll never tell him that. I know about sex because I've seen it before. I've seen it up close; the beads of sweat that formed along Father's back, and the way his buttcheeks would clench every time he'd thrust into Mommy. She was a lot hairier between her legs than the woman in the magazine, and her breasts were smaller.

She was natural, and this woman isn't.

As I chew the last bite of my sandwich, I push the magazine away and ignore them.

"Fucking freak." Clay laughs, flicking my ear.

They're trying to get a reaction out of me, but I won't give them one. If I do, they'll only torment me even worse. The last time I made the mistake of engaging with them by standing up for myself, the three of them dragged me into the bathroom and forced my head into the dirty toilet. My nostrils burned, and the water came out of my nose after I choked and swallowed it.

They're looking for a reason to continue toying with me, baiting me, but I'll never again make the mistake of showing them how I really feel.

I'm glad Father taught me that lesson. That's the only thing I learned from the jerk.

Standing, I walk away without making eye contact, giving them my back as they continue with their insults and shit talking, their laughter fading into the background the farther I get away from them.

When I'm outside and away from my terrible foster brothers, I hear quiet sobs and sniffles. My chest aches, the hair on my arms standing straight up as goosebumps form.

I know it's her without even seeing her.

There's no way to explain it, and I don't understand it, but I feel in sync with the blue-eyed girl. I can feel her sadness and can tell what she's thinking or feeling just by looking into her bottomless eyes. It's strange, but I feel like she's my soulmate.

I've had dreams about her. When I dream, I'm in a different body and so is she. We're not stuck in this house, we're different people, living in a different time.

It makes little sense and maybe one day I'll understand it.

Once I saw a movie about soulmates and reincarnation. It seemed like a silly thing mother loved, but when I'd asked, she told me that soulmates exist and when you find your mate, you'll continue to find each other in many lifetimes all over again. She said it's deeper than love, but when I asked if Father was her soulmate, she never gave me an answer.

I think Lee is mine.

Her figure comes into view as I turn the corner, watching her as she sits in the grass, her knees to her chest, her head bowed as she uses the sleeves of her sweater to viciously wipe her tears away.

Her light eyebrows are pulled together in a scowl, as if she's angry at herself for crying.

Before she sees me, I slip away, returning to the front of the house right to where Marla keeps her prized rosebush perfectly trimmed and on display.

The perfect rosebush looks funny compared to the half-dead grass and raggedy green house with brown shutters and a screen door that's one good slam away from coming off its hinges.

Marla loves these damn roses and yells at us anytime we get too close to them, but that doesn't stop me from finding the perfect, fully bloomed red rose and clipping it from the bush along with the thorns using the pruning shears she keeps in a bucket nearby along with her gardening gloves.

I think Marla only enjoys having the rose bush because she doesn't have a man in her life buying her flowers. Not that I blame a single man out there. She's a troll with an equally ugly and bitchy personality.

Who wants to come home to that every day?

With the rose in hand, I march toward Lee, looking down at her as I stand in front of her.

Her blonde head pops up, surprise and sadness in her clear eyes as she stares up at me.

"Hi, Ace." She sniffles, wiping the remaining tears from her face.

I don't enjoy seeing her cry. She's too pretty for tears, and I vow that as long as I live, I will do everything in my power to put a smile on her face and never let her cry again like she is now.

She gazes in amazement as I hold the rose out to her, her eyes darting between the flawless flower and myself.

"Is this from Marla's rosebush?" She eyes it skeptically. I can tell she wants it but won't allow herself to have it. She's being cautious, and she should be, but not with me. I'd never set her up.

Nodding and stepping closer, I wave it in front of her face, willing her to take it.

Her eyes display her internal battle. She wants it, but she's afraid. With a sigh of defeat, she reaches up and takes the rose from my outstretched hand, her soft fingers touching my skin. The small two-second touch sends shockwaves through my body, somehow mending my broken heart.

"Why are you giving this to me?" she asks, bringing the flower to her small button nose, inhaling its floral scent deeply.

She cradles it in her hands, holding it like it's the most precious gift she's ever received.

Finally, a smile replaces the sadness in her eyes and her glow is back, showing me she really is the bright light in the middle of all this madness.

I've never been much of a talker, but for the first time, I want to carry on a conversation with her. The urge to speak and have someone listen to everything I have to say overwhelms me.

Staring into her pretty eyes, I speak to her for the first time, "Pretty things deserve pretty things."

Her cute button nose scrunches up, a pink blush stinging her tear-stained cheeks.

"Why were you crying?"

Hugging the rose to her chest, she exhales before opening her mouth to speak, but whatever she was about to say dies on her lips at the sights of Marla's silver Toyota Camry pulling into the driveway, ruining the first moment I've had alone with the pretty golden girl.

Later that night, Marla took the belt to me for plucking one of her roses, but it was worth it. I didn't apologize, instead I took the beating with a smile.

Even when Lee snuck into the bathroom with me afterward and helped me rub ointment on the welts on my back, my smile never once faded.

Little did I know that she'd be gone a few months later, and I'd spend the rest of my life obsessed with her.

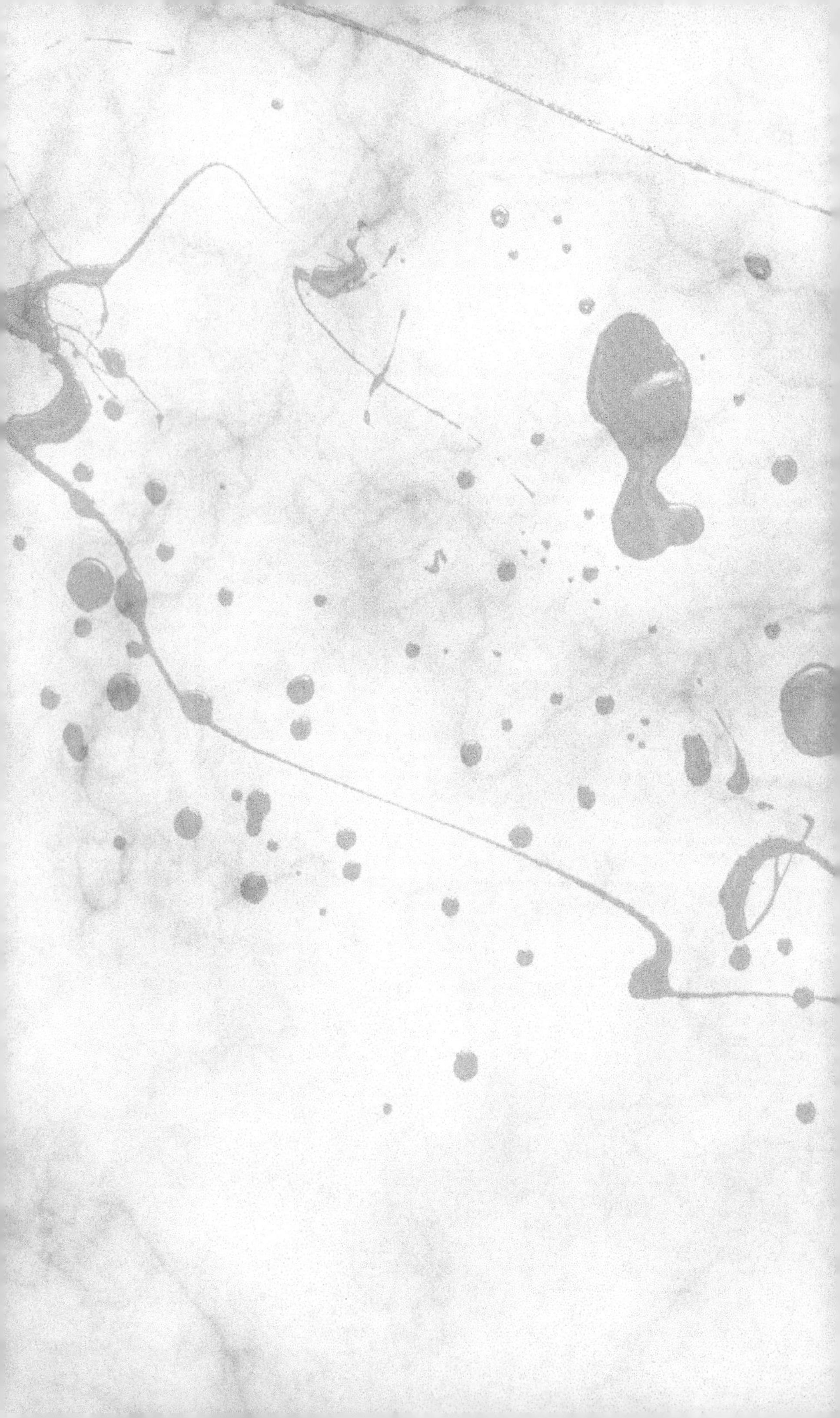

Chapter Five

THIRTEEN YEARS OLD

TODAY IS MY THIRTEENTH BIRTHDAY, AND NO ONE KNOWS. Well, someone knows, but the person I want to see the most isn't around me anymore. The pretty girl with golden hair is gone, and I don't know where she went.

They made her leave. She was mine, and they took her from me.

I guess it doesn't matter because two weeks after her departure; they sent me to a new home.

According to Marla, I was too much of a freak that made her feel uncomfortable, and she no longer wanted me in the house. Stacey, my caseworker, picked me up, and two hours later I was on a new doorstep.

Margot has been my new foster mom for a few months now, and I don't like her or anyone in this house. I prefer Marla's house.

Everyone always takes my stuff in this house.

Like my art supplies.

Margot locked my stuff away in the garage, but she doesn't know that I can pick a lock and plan on getting it back once she leaves for the day.

Every Saturday at noon she leaves to get her hair and nails done, and luckily for me, she'll be leaving soon, and I'll be able to break into her lockbox in the garage and get my stuff back. No one has any fucking right taking what's mine.

It's not considered stealing because it's my belongings that she took from me. I'm simply taking back what's mine.

I wait until I hear the old creaking front door close, then I stand from my twin bed and leave my room, walking into the living room.

From where I stand in front of the window, I watch Margot's car pull out of the driveway and disappear down the street.

She won't be back until late, and she'll smell like booze when she gets home. I know she'll go straight to bed. This is why I love Saturdays.

Like Marla, Margot takes in foster children only for the checks, and she doesn't care about us. Sometimes she's nicer than Marla, at least when she's not taking my stuff. Most of the time, she allows me to go outside and do anything I want as long as I'm good.

I'm always good.

Except for two weeks ago, which is why she took my art supplies in the first place.

Two weeks ago, it was Lee's birthday, and all I wanted was to see her or know that she was okay at whatever new home she ended up at. I begged Margot to let me call Stacey and ask for an update, but she denied me. In a fit of rage, I called her a bitch, stormed into my bedroom, and slammed the door.

I was in the middle of drawing yet another portrait of Lee when Margot, the stupid troll, ripped the photo away, so I threw a pencil at her. I'm positive it didn't hurt, but she still screamed at me and took my sketchpads and pencils, anyway.

Stupid bitch.

The art set was a gift from Stacey a couple months ago when she came for a visit and noticed I'd become interested in drawing. She thought it was great that I'd found a way to express myself, so the next time she came, she brought sketchpads and a set of sketching pencils. It was the nicest thing I owned, and I cherished it, taking care of it as if my life depended on it. Those items are the only things I own that are truly mine. They're brand new.

Since the day I ended up in foster care with only the clothes on my back, all they had ever given me were used items. Used shoes that were too small—to the point that I had to duct tape back together. Pants that were too short for my long legs. Faded T-shirts that don't fit properly. No one at my public school makes fun of me, probably because most of them are dressed similarly. It's obvious my school is for the group of unwanted kids and low-income families.

I've been on my best behavior for the past few weeks, trying to show Margot that I deserve to have my things returned. If it weren't for my irritating foster sister, Ashley, I would have had them back by now.

Margot had agreed that I'd been good and said she'd give me my stuff back three days ago, but when Ashley heard that, she lied, saying I'd ripped up her homework and because of me she'd fail the assignment. Truth is, she hadn't done her homework, but as payback, Margot said she will not give me back my art set.

I'm not too fond of either of them right now.

Had Ashley not been a dirty little liar, I'd have my art supplies, and wouldn't be grounded. Because of her, my precious art kit is locked away in the garage, taunting me.

At first, I wasn't sure where Margot had put it, but the other day she caught Ashley with a case full of makeup and took it from her, and I saw her put it in the lockbox in the garage, right next to my art case.

When Margot took the makeup from Ashley, I had to excuse myself and go into my bedroom because I couldn't stop laughing. Ashley can wear all the makeup she wants, but she will never stop being the ugly hag she is. Somehow, those products only showcase the worst parts of her face.

Once I'm certain Margot is gone, I creep into the garage without making a sound. Sunlight from the crack underneath the garage door peeks in, providing enough light for me to locate exactly what I'm looking for.

Luckily for me, Margot didn't hide her lockbox of stolen items, and apart from a few plastic storage containers lined up on the metal shelves against the wall, the garage is clear. At this moment, I'm glad for Margot's need to keep everything neat and organized in her home. There's never a single item out of place.

We're alike in that way. I enjoy having things neat. Mess and being unorganized causes me to feel stressed, and makes my mind feel jumbled.

I'm already not in control of my life but having things neat and in order at least allow me to control one part of my life, which is why when Margot assigns the weekly chore chart, I don't mind that I always do more than Ashley.

My plan was to pick the lock to get my art supplies, but as I stand in front of the large wooden chest on the floor of the garage, my anger rises, and suddenly, I don't care about Margot finding out what I'm doing or not. She'll find out eventually anyway—as soon as she opens the chest and discovers my belongings are missing but Ashley's remain.

Instead, I grab a hammer from the shelf and smash the lock, hitting it repeatedly until the metal breaks away. Kicking it to the side, I open the lid of the chest, relief instantly washing over me at the sight of my sketchpad and pack of sketching pencils.

The sight has me breathing easier, and a weight somehow feels lifted from my shoulders. This is what I needed.

With the items in hand, I go into the kitchen, flipping to the most recent page I'd been on when Margot had taken it.

Sitting at the table, I open the pencil case, remove the black pencil, and begin shading in the image, going right back to where I had been.

Calmness stills my racing mind, my heartbeat returning to normal.

After thirty minutes, I set it aside and venture toward the pantry in search of a snack, landing on apples and peanut butter. Another thing I like about Margot is she doesn't mind us helping ourselves to the food in the kitchen. She doesn't grocery shop often, but she lets us eat whatever we want.

Grabbing a paring knife and cutting board, I set them on the counter and begin peeling the apple, removing the red skin.

"Is that your stupid art book? How the hell did you get it?" Ashley sneers, her arms crossing over her chest and eyes squinting as she looks between the open sketchpad on the table and me.

I ignore her, keeping my hands steady as I slice up an apple to eat with the creamy peanut butter I love. Margot finally bought it. She typically gets the chunky kind, and I hate it. I feel special when she buys things I like.

"Hello?!" Ashley stomps her foot, stepping closer to me, snapping her fingers in front of my face. "I'm telling Margot that you stole from her. You're going to be in so much trouble. I hope she kicks you out like the trash you are." She laughs. "No wonder your parents gave you away. I bet they hated you just like everyone else probably hates you. No wonder you don't have any friends," she mocks, her evil high-pitched laughter becoming the only sound I'm able to hear.

My breathing becomes slow and shallow as pressure builds in

my chest, tingles shooting up and down my spine. Her cruel words are nothing new, and typically I never let her see how much she affects me, but today I can't seem to ignore her. Her cruelness never bothers me, but today is my birthday, and I'm alone.

"Oh wait, whoops, I forgot your mom died." I make the mistake of finally looking over my shoulder at her, making eye contact. For a moment I think she's going to apologize or at least leave me alone, but of course that would be too kind for her. She doesn't have a kind bone in her body. She's evil, and there's no hope for people like her.

"Shut up, Ashley." My shoulders slouch in defeat. I hate myself for letting her see the affect her words have on me.

Ashley steps closer to me, pressing her body firmly against the side of me. Beads of sweat form along my hairline at the physical contact. Watching her from the corner of my eye, I witness her leaning in close to me, her breath warm against my neck as goosebumps cover my body.

"Your mother died because she hated you so much that death was the only way to be free of you," she whispers, her lips dancing across my skin at the closeness of her. "You are nothing, Ace. You're a freak and should do everyone a favor and kill yourself." My hands shake, my brows furrowing in confusion.

How can her words be so cruel, yet my body is reacting somehow to the closeness of her and the feel of her warm breath on my neck? My mind and body are sending each other mixed signals.

"Shut up. Please, just shut up and get away from me," I beg, letting my heavy eyelids close, my lips parting as my breathing becomes uneven and raspy.

Laughter fills my ears as she finally takes a step back, the fog clearing from my brain with the more distance she creates between us.

"Aww, are you going to cry? Let me get a good look at you so I can savor this moment." Her fingers wrap around my forearm, pulling me away from the counter until I'm facing her. I'm stronger than her and could've easily resisted, but I never do when it comes to her or anyone else. I let everyone walk all over me all the time and never do a damn thing about it.

She's wrong, though. I will not cry. I'm angry. So fucking angry and tired of being pushed around by everyone in my life. Those around me laugh at me at my expense and I've done nothing to stop it. I'm a doormat, just like Father once told me. People walk all over me and push me because I allow it.

Not anymore. I'm done being pathetic.

"Watch your fucking mouth, Ashley, or I swear to God—"

"What? What will you do, freak?" she challenges, standing toe-to-toe with me. She's much shorter than me and has to tilt her head back to look at me while I stare down at her, looking into her blue eyes.

Her eyes are boring, unlike my pretty thing, whose blue eyes hold the key to the world's greatest mysteries. Everything about Ashley is simple. Nothing about her is special.

My trembling hands ball into fists at my side, my right hand tightening around the handle of the knife I'd been using to slice my apple. I hadn't realized that it's still in my hand, but now I'm not willing to let go of it.

Anger unlike I've ever felt before flows through my veins, making my heartbeat so rapidly I'm afraid it'll beat out of my chest.

She takes my silence as her victory, a smirk spreading across her pink lips. "Whatever, freak." She shakes her head, her blonde ponytail shaking. "Take your shit and go into your room and draw your stupid-ass pictures." Her eyes flick from me to the table where my sketchpad lies open on the drawing that I'd been drawing a few weeks ago when Margot had taken it.

It's a picture of her. Every page in the book is a picture of her.

The girl with a halo of hair, turquoise eyes that got brighter when I was around. My pretty thing. The girl I've been dreaming about since the day I laid eyes on her.

"Whoever that girl is, good thing she got away from you." Her attention turns back to me, eyes full of mischief. "Does she know what a freak you really are?" She taps her chin with her pink fingernail as if she's deep in thought. "Hmm, I wonder if she's the reason you were moved here. Did you hurt her?" she gasps, and I can practically see the invisible lightbulb above her head lighting up.

"Oh my God, that's exactly what happened, isn't it? Let me guess, she was your foster sister at your last home, but your freakish self-snuck into her room after foster mommy and daddy went to sleep? You watched her in the shower, too, like you watch me."

"Shut the fuck up, Ashley!" I yell, surprising us both at the boom of my voice. I never raise my voice. Ever. I'm the quiet one. I always have been.

"I'm telling Margot what a freak you are."

"You don't know anything!"

"Freak! Freak! Freak!" she taunts, laughing in my face as if working me up and using Lee against me is the funniest thing in the world.

Without thinking, I act on impulse and lunge at her. "Shut up! Shut up! Shut up!" I yell, shoving her forcefully away from me.

The room becomes silent, and I watch as Ashley's eyes widen, her hands moving to her stomach.

The air in the kitchen becomes heavy, my chest rising and falling rapidly as I watch her movements, watching her pull her hand away from her stomach to reveal the crimson liquid covering her palm.

"W-w-what did you do?" she stutters, looking at her hands in utter disbelief, her eyes as wide as saucers.

Oh my God. What did I do?

Holding my breath, my eyes turn from her, and I look at my right hand. I'm holding a knife that is now covered in blood.

"Ashley, I'm so sorry. I didn't mean to." Tears sting my eyes. I'm going to be in so much trouble. It was an accident, but that won't matter.

"I'm calling Margot. You need to be locked up, freak!" She hiccups, turning her back on me as she hunches forward, holding her stomach.

I've always been told I was a bad boy and a freak. Maybe everyone is right. Maybe I am bad because what I want to do to her makes me feel calm.

Stabbing her the first time was an accident, but walking over to her and plunging the knife into her back isn't an accident.

Her small body collapses to the floor with a thump, her chest rising and falling rapidly as she lies on her back, her wide eyes full of tears.

"This is your fault, Ashley. You should've shut your mouth." For the first time in a while, I feel calm. The euphoria that courses through my body is the same feeling I had when I witnessed my mother die.

My pants grow tighter as my body reacts to the scene before me, an uncontrolled smile spreading across my lips.

Fear no longer controls me, instead, all I want to do is experience more of the beautiful crimson that's currently pooling out of her body. Instead of holding myself back, I allow myself to give in to the urges and allow the bliss to consume me.

Dropping to my knees beside her, I raise the knife above her chest and bring it down with force. A laugh erupts from my parted lips as I remove the blade and stab her repeatedly.

The room is filled with the sounds of my heavy breathing and the wet squelch of the blade going in and out of her flesh.

I don't stop until my arms are aching, and I'm out of breath. Sitting beside her, I stare at her lifeless, mutilated body until my breathing evens, and I'm able to muster up enough strength to stand on my legs.

Margot will be home soon, and this is what she'll find. I'll be arrested for murder and locked up, just like everyone always told me I will be.

Ashley's blood splatter coats my skin, my hands covered in the beautiful crimson, the knife still held tight in my fist. I have limited time alone. Margot will surely be home soon, but the threat of her seeing me isn't enough to stop me from doing what I must do.

Opening my fist, the knife drops to the floor with a thud, landing with a splatter in the pool of blood. My calm fingers work the buttons on my jeans, and within seconds I have my hard cock freed from the denim and have it securely inside my bloody fist.

My focus never strays from the body in front of me as I pump my hand over my shaft, applying pressure each time I get to the tip. My body shakes with euphoria, the feeling consuming me until the point I give in and feel the tingles as they begin climbing up my spine.

Dropping to my knees beside Ashley's head, I continue my jerky strokes, a strangled groan climbing up the back of my throat as I explode, spraying thick coats of cum on her face.

A satisfied smile spreads along my lips as my digits carefully trace over the white fluid dripping down her cheek and swipe it up into her mouth. "Karma is a bitch, Ashley, just like you." Once I've gotten most of my fluid into her mouth, I stand and stare at her, admiring the masterpiece spread out before me.

The blood on my arms begins to itch as it dries, and before I go to jail, I'd like to wash myself.

I've seen prison movies before. I know they don't get to take their time and enjoy a hot shower. We have that in common, because I've never been able to take a long, hot shower either.

With Ashley's corpse in the kitchen, I go into the bathroom, remove my clothes, and take an hour-long shower, scrubbing every inch of my body until I'm positive her blood is gone.

Once I'm out, I dress myself in my favorite outfit. It's a simple T-shirt and jeans, but they're in good condition and don't have any holes or stains. Good thing I wasn't wearing them earlier. I would've hated to ruin them with the blood of that witch.

I'm prepared to call 911 myself, but as I return to the kitchen where the house phone is located, the sight of my sketchpad stops me in my tracks.

My pretty thing.

If I'm in jail, who will watch after her?

We may be separated now, but that's temporary. If I'm locked up, I'll never get back to her.

She's the most important person in my life, and I won't let her down.

Instead of doing the right thing, I sneak into Margot's room and take the emergency fund that she keeps in a Ziploc bag under her mattress. I know it's there because I found it one weekend while I was meddling in her room after I moved in. I'd been curious, so I snooped.

After packing a backpack with everything I own, along with six hundred dollars in my pocket and nowhere to go, I run.

I disappear into the stillness of the night, running as far away from that house and my crime as I can, looking over my shoulder and hiding behind bushes every time I hear a car pass me by.

I'm not sure what'll happen, but for now, I'm going to find her.

[illegible]

[illegible]

[illegible]

[illegible]

[illegible]

[illegible]

Chapter Six

TWENTY-FOUR YEARS OLD

MY PARENTS WERE WRONG WHEN THEY TOLD ME THERE WAS no God. For years I looked over my shoulder, worried that the past would catch up to me and I'd be punished for what I did that day to Ashley. Except that day never came, and I'm still here, free. If that's not a sign that God exists, I don't know what is.

No one cared that a fourteen-year-old foster child was murdered, the prime suspect being her thirteen-year-old foster brother who disappeared that same night. I searched every newspaper I came across for updates, but one day, two weeks later, the stories about Ashley stopped.

The police stopped caring, and I could breathe a little easier and sleep a little better at night. It's sad, really. She was a person who, because of me, will never get to grow up and have a future. I stole that from her without a care in the world. I get to live my life, and she doesn't. You'd think that someone out there would care, but no one does anymore. I've walked by Margot's house a few times since then, and she continues to have a regular turning wheel of kids coming in and out of her home.

Surely her license should've been revoked considering a kid died in her home on her watch, but that just goes to show how little anyone cares about the children in the system. She gets more children and checks, and life goes on as if a girl hadn't lost her life.

Half of me feels guilty, and the other half feels relief for doing what I did. The voices in my head calmed down that day, but that was also the day I realized more than ever that there's something wrong with me.

I'd questioned it since I was a little boy. Blood and gore have always fascinated me.

When I was younger, I would turn on R-rated movies, typically horror movies, after my parents went to sleep and sit in front of the television, as close as I could get, and watch in awe as the killer's knife would pierce their victim's skin, blood pouring out of their wound.

Obviously, I'm aware it was fake, but I've never been able to get those images out of my head or stop wondering what it would feel like if the knife were in my hands. My fascination only grew when I witnessed my mother's death, and watched the life slowly leave her brown eyes as she took her final breath, blood pooling from her body.

Maybe Sharon was right when she said I have the devil in me and maybe Father was right all those times he told me I was a bad boy.

Did I deserve all those punishments? I never thought I was bad until now. I hate Father for all he did to me over the years, but did he see something in me I'm not yet aware of?

The first time he came into my bedroom to deliver my punishment was after I'd left my backpack and homework scattered on the living room coffee table. He'd been away all day, working late, so mother and I ate dinner without him, which was something we rarely did. Father always got angry at her when we ate without him, but it was after eight and I was starving, so she said we could eat.

That night, I was sound asleep in my twin-sized bed, hugging my blue racecar blanket against my chest when he came in smelling of alcohol and pulled my pajama pants down. For several minutes, he told me I was a bad boy, telling me bad boys deserve to be punished.

The next day, Mommy kept me home from school, let me eat ice cream for breakfast, and bought me a remote-controlled race car. Father said nothing about my punishment, and for the next few weeks, he ignored me as he typically did.

I was a good boy for four weeks, then one day I was bad and received another punishment. It didn't take long for it to become a regular occurrence, but one day, Mommy told me I wasn't a bad boy and said she could make me feel better. She wanted me to feel loved and not so sad after Father's punishments. That was the first day she put her mouth between my legs and showed me how it felt to be loved.

Father would tell me I was bad; Mother would tell me I was good.

For years, I felt conflicted. Am I a good boy? Or am I a bad boy?

The question weighed heavy on my mind for years. As much as I wanted to believe I was good, that I am good, I'm questioning myself and always have.

Sharon agreed with Father that I was bad, so if two people were saying it, is it true? Look at what I did to Ashley. That's not something a good boy would do.

The thoughts I have don't make me feel good either.

How can I control what's inside of me? It feels like a monster is living inside of me. And the only time I've ever felt like I have tamed it is when I met her. The girl with golden hair and eyes as blue as the ocean I hope to experience in person one day.

The question of good and bad is one that I'll have conflict over for the rest of my life.

For a while, I felt good when I was with her.

It took some time, but I eventually found Lee. I saved her, or so I thought. I sent her to my Aunt Willa, who promised to care for her.

That story has already been told, so I won't get into it again, but that ended up being a complete shit show, and something I'll regret for the rest of my life.

Now, she's gone and wants to be free of me. She wants a chance to live a life of her own and get to make her own decisions for the first time, but I can't allow that.

She needs me. She'll always need me, which is why I've been looking after her since we parted ways that day at Rachel's house after Olivia's birth.

I'm looking after her the best way I can, even though I know it's wrong to stalk someone.

It's wrong to hide in the shadows, watching someone's every move, ducking behind a building or car whenever they look over their shoulder.

My pretty thing knows she's being watched. I know she's aware because every so often she looks over her shoulder as if she can feel me watching her. Feel my breath on the back of her neck. Feel my heartbeat pressed against her back. Or feel my eyes on her skin during the times I've hidden in her closet and watched her.

We're connected, so I know she can feel me. Honestly, I think she enjoys being watched. Enjoys knowing that I'm only a scream away.

It's a never-ending game, and I love playing with her.

Lee thinks she can have space and time away from me, but

she doesn't understand that we're two halves of the same soul. We're soulmates, and no matter where she tries to run and hide, she'll never be able to escape me.

Not even in death will she be able to escape me. I'll find her again and again, in every single lifetime.

For years, she's been dragging me along, giving me bits and pieces of herself, and like the lovesick fool I am, I crave the crumbs she gives me. It'll never be enough, but I know that one day, even once I have all of her, I'll never be able to reach my fill. In every lifetime that'll come after this, my soul will find hers, and we'll repeat this game again.

Our bodies may change, but our souls will live on forever.

We're connected as one, and you cannot live without your soul.

I gave up trying to live without her when I was twelve years old, and since then, I've been chasing the scraps of attention I can get from her.

When she was seventeen and pregnant, I thought that would be our chance to be together, but I was a fool that should've known better. She wasn't ready yet, and every day since then I've been waiting for her to be ready.

Good thing I'm a patient man, because I'm willing to wait as long as it takes for her to realize we're inevitable and will be together for eternity.

She is my life. I exist solely for the purpose of obsessing over her.

I'd say love, but love feels too insignificant for what I feel for her. Love is too minor of a word to describe my obsession. My need.

Over the years, I've watched her as much as possible. There were moments when we lost time because of circumstances outside of my control, but now that I have her back in my sights, there's no escaping me again.

She can ask for all the space and time apart she wants but look what happened last time. It's my fault they hurt her. Lee trusted me, and I trusted Willa, when I should've been the one to watch after her myself, because there's not a soul on this planet that can care for her the way I do.

That is why I remain in the shadows, watching her from a distance, because I never want to be responsible for her being in harm's way again.

My need to watch her is what led me here tonight, to Ciel Ballet.

My pretty thing is performing tonight, and I haven't missed one performance in six months. Watching her dance is the highlight of my life. It's the brightest time of my day. The only thing that brings happiness in my dark, miserable life.

Seeing her on stage, gliding around gracefully, doing the thing she loves with a smile on her face brings me joy, and it's the reason I stay out of sight, allowing her to live her life.

It kills me to not be able to sit in the front row with roses in hand, clapping and cheering the loudest for her, waiting for when she gets off stage so I can wrap my arms around her petite body and show her how much I love her. I fantasize about what her expression would be if she looked out into the audience and saw me sitting there. Her eyes would light up, a wide smile would spread across her plump pink lips, and then she'd run to me, thanking me for being there for her and would kiss me, getting so lost in our passion that we'd momentarily forget about the rest of the audience.

As much as I want to be, I'm not the reason she smiles when she looks out into the audience. From where I sit in the back of the darkened room, hidden in the crowd, I witness her eyes scan the audience, and I know the exact moment her focus lands on the person she wants to see. The smile that stretches across her face infuriates me, and nearly has me ready to jump out of my seat, wanting to rush toward the man responsible for that smile on her heart-shaped face.

Sebastian.

The man she met three months ago is responsible for all her smiles lately. I've asked around about him, even used my growing computer skills to dig into him, and every person and article I found about the man has been positive. No one has a bad thing to say about the man who saves lives.

The local newspaper had an article on him a few weeks ago because he made a large donation to a homeless shelter, along with volunteering when he had free time. I wonder what he'd think if he knew the woman he knows isn't who she says she is. She's not the perfect girl I created her to be, and I wonder how he'd feel about her if he really knew all the things she'd experienced.

Would he think she was damaged goods?

Would he love her even more because of her flaws and scars?

I know everything about her, and I'd never leave her. I love her even more because of the things she's been through in her young twenty-one years of life.

Everything he knows about her is a lie, and one day I fear her lies will come crashing down around her. When that happens, I'll be there to catch her.

I'm always there to catch her and pick up the pieces. She's just as broken as I am, and that's why we belong together. I recognized her broken pieces the first day I met her and looked into her captivating blue eyes.

After the show ends, I remain seated, watching as other guests clear out of the room, while others stick around to greet the dancers they know.

My pretty thing is the last to appear from behind the black door that's off toward the side of the stage. The air shifts with her appearance. Everyone else in the room seems to disappear, and it's only the two of us.

My focus is on her until Sebastian suddenly blocks my view. Yet again, I must remind myself that she's with him right now and doesn't know I'm even here.

This is what she wants, and I shouldn't be angry, but how can I not be? She's my soul, and instead of us being together, she's parading around with another man. It's my fault, really. I allowed her to have space away from me.

Lee's face lights up, and she runs into his arms, wrapping herself around him like she's done it a thousand times before.

Only this time, I noticed something I hadn't noticed before, a diamond ring on her left ring finger.

She hadn't been wearing it when she was dancing, or the last time I seen her, which means it's new, and he's given it to her recently.

What the actual fuck?

An engagement ring.

She agreed to marry this loser.

My hands ball into fists at my sides, my vision becoming blurry with rage as I stare at the seemingly happy couple, my stomach tightening and knotting. Bile threatens to claw its way up my throat, but I swallow it back.

How could she? How fucking could she?

I stand there, watching them, until they eventually leave with his arm around her shoulders as he guides her out of the building. All while, that diamond ring shines and taunts me.

I came here tonight to watch her dance, and instead I'm leaving with a broken heart.

She's making it hard to keep the faith that we'll be together.

One day, she'll regret it. I'll make sure of it.

Once in the parking lot, I run to my car, barely making it to the door by the time the bile I'd swallowed earlier climbs back up and forces me to hunch over and vomit my guts out on the pavement.

I wipe my mouth once I'm certain there's nothing left in my stomach to upchuck. Then I drive away, trying but failing to put the image of that ring out of my mind.

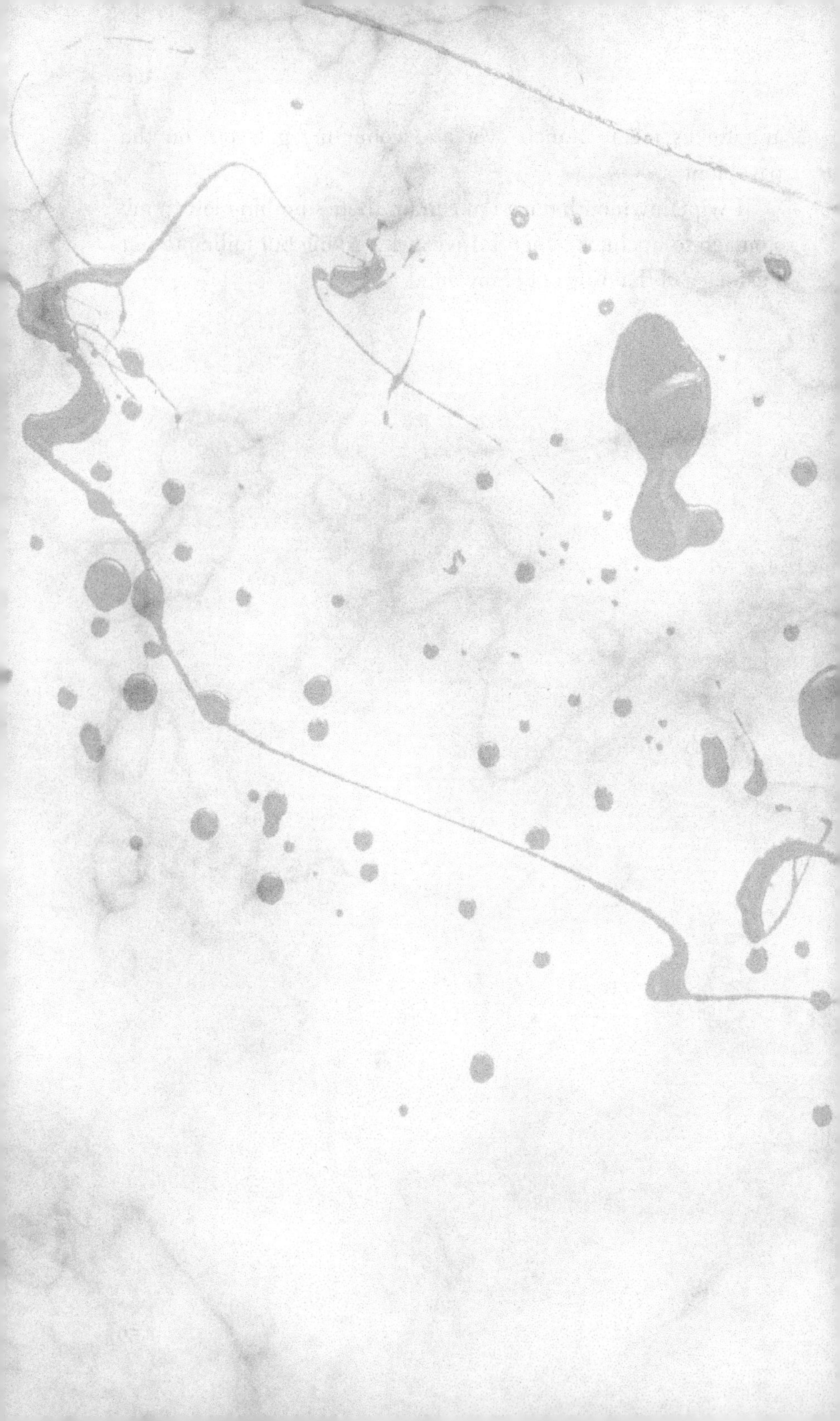

Chapter Seven

When I was nine years old, one night during dinner, I asked my parents about sex. I'd seen them together that way many times before, but they called it "making love." They always told me that's how you show someone you love them.

It's special and you should only make love to the person you marry because that's who you'll spend the rest of your life with.

They'd tell me the same thing every single time.

I'd never known that making love was the same as sex. Father washed my mouth out with a bar of soap and hot sauce and made me promise to never use that filthy word again.

"Sex is for whores. Making love is for two people who love each other."

As I got older, I learned more and more about sex.

I'd met no one that I wanted to share that part of myself with until her, and unfortunately that'll have to wait. I was going to save myself for her, because I don't want any other woman in this world to have that part of myself.

There's only one woman I want to bury myself inside. And when I finally get the chance, I plan to bury myself so fucking deep inside of her she'll never be able to figure out where I end and she begins.

If she continues playing games with me, I may cut her open, climb inside of her body, and wear her skin like latex. She'll never be able to get rid of me.

We will become one.

One day, she'll pay for what she did tonight.

Seeing her kiss Sebastian made me feel like my heart was being ripped from my chest. The thought of him getting down on one knee and proposing to my pretty thing after only three months together has me holding my breath until my head feels dizzy.

By agreeing to marry him, Lee became a bad girl. And bad girls get punished. One day, she'll feel the burn the same way I feel the burn in my chest, knowing she's wearing his ring.

She agreed to marry him.

How can she do that to me? I spend every day thinking of her while she's living her best life, not thinking of me at all. Yes, I want her to live a glorious life because she deserves it, but she also deserves to be miserable without me.

I have faith that one day she'll return to me when the stars align and it's our time to be together permanently, but her agreeing to marry another man puts a big fucking hole in my plans. Once she becomes his wife, he'll never let her go, and I know this because once she's officially mine, I won't ever let her go either.

My aching heart drove me to International Boulevard, the part of town known for sex work.

I've saved myself for her, but tonight I realized it's pointless. I'm unsure if they've already been having sex. Though, I can only hope like hell that they haven't. Once they're married, I know for certain that they will be. There's no way in hell Sebastian can be married to her and living with her and not sink himself inside of her perfect pussy.

Lucky fucker.

He'll have another piece of what's mine if he hasn't already. He'll have something that I've yet to have.

I blame my pretty thing for making me want to do something that I've never wanted to do before. Before tonight, I would've been fine with keeping myself pure for her, but now, I want to experience what it's like to be buried so fucking deep inside of a woman.

Being a virgin at twenty-four never bothered me, but now I'm ready to fuck someone out of spite. I'll find a whore to satisfy me, and I'll become dirty.

With my windows rolled down, I park at the corner, watching the parade of women walking up and down the streets, watching as they get in and out of cars, watching others exchange money on the streets. I feel dirty just being here, and even angrier that Lee is forcing me to be here.

All she had to do was refuse his proposal. Instead, she accepted, causing my hope for us to dwindle. I know I said I was a patient man, but how much does she expect me to fucking put up with?

My beautiful little bitch. Spreading her legs like a whore.

I've ignored my body anytime it's reacted to a beautiful woman. I've kept my hands to myself or went some place private to stroke my cock while visions of Lee played in my head. The point is, I never once would've thought about touching another woman.

Until now.

This is her fucking fault. I'm going to ruin myself because of her.

I tell myself I'll only do it once, and for my sake, I hope it's true.

"Hey, baby, you looking for some company?" A woman's voice pulls me away from my thoughts and back into reality. The strange woman leans down to my open passenger window with a smirk on her hot pink over-lined painted lips.

Straightening in my seat, I shove my shaky hands between my thighs, forcing myself to give her a smile. "Sure am." I can do this. It's just sex. It'll mean nothing, and I only have to do it once.

"You're in luck, handsome. I can give you the time of your life." She squeezes her arms together, her cleavage becoming more prominent in the gold bikini top she's wearing.

I gulp, keeping my eyes on her face rather than her breasts. She wants me to look, but that would be disrespectful when we're having a conversation. "I h-h-have a motel room around the corner," I stutter, like the immature man child I feel like I am. The pornographic videos I've been watching recently didn't prepare me for this moment.

"Not so fast, Romeo. What are you looking for, exactly?"

"U-u-uh," I stutter. Fuck, this isn't going as I had planned in my head.

This wasn't how it was in *Pretty Woman.*

The woman laughs, opening the door. "This must be your first time. Don't worry, baby, I'll take good care of you. Do you have cash?"

I nod, watching in silence as she climbs into my passenger seat. "Good. Let's go to your room, and I'll make you feel good." Her tan hand reaches across and rests on my thigh, her long pink acrylic nails inching closer and closer toward my crotch, my cock jerking at the sudden feel of another person touching it.

It's been years since someone touched me there, but before I lose the nerve and start panicking like a little bitch, I shift the car into drive with shaky hands and follow the speed limit for the ten-minute drive to Willow Motel where I'm staying for the night.

The room I rented is for this purpose only. I'm already doing something impure. I wasn't about to take her to my apartment, my only safe space in the world.

Once we're in the room, the woman, who introduced herself as Candy during the drive, struts in on her six-inch gold heels as if she owns the place. Her ass cheeks peek out of her little black leather shorts, revealing long tan legs, that I suddenly can't wait to have wrapped around me.

I wonder if she'll be as sweet as her name is.

Who names their child Candy?

The thought surprises me, but I can't deny the physical attraction my body has to her. She's a beautiful woman and looks like she knows how to take care of a man.

"You've never done this before, have you?" She breaks the silence as she stops in front of the king-sized bed and faces me.

Shyly, I remain rooted in place by the door, shifting the locks in place. The room smells musty, and the faded yellow walls and stained carpets have seen better days, but this is the only place that accepts cash by the hour without needing identification. It's not exactly what I had in mind for my first time, but it's got a bed which is all I need.

Remembering her question, my eyes land on Candy. Several breaths pass between us before I'm able to slowly nod, confirming what she asked. She's a professional, of course she's able to tell that I'm a virgin.

"Come over here and lie down. I'll make you feel good." She holds her hand out toward me. My feet have a mind of their own and move in her direction as my hand reaches out to accept hers.

Her skin is soft beneath my fingertips, but looking at her feels wrong. Everything about her is wrong.

From the blues eyes to the blonde hair and milky skin, it's all wrong. She's not the one I want. The woman I want is across town with her fiancé.

Instead, I found this blue-eyed woman as a surrogate for the one I really want but can't yet have.

"You have pretty eyes," I compliment her, and her hands move to my chest, slipping underneath my shirt as her fingernails graze my skin.

"You have weird eyes," she remarks, commenting on my heterochromia. I have one blue eye and one brown. Everyone has always told me it's weird, and according to Sharon, it's proof that I have the devil in me. Maybe she's right, because the more I look at the woman in front of me, the more I realize that I want to watch her bleed the same way I watched Ashley bleed out in front of me.

Candy's hands on my body don't get my dick hard. Even as she removes my clothing and begins stroking me, I remain still, completely flaccid.

The only thing that causes my dick to jerk to life is the realization that I enjoyed watching Ashley die, and I want to witness it again. Even as much as I miss my mother and loved her deeply, I enjoyed watching her beautiful blood leave her body and life leave her eyes.

I'm fucked up. Completely fucked up.

The devil is real, and he's inside of me.

At some point while I'm trapped in my thoughts I must've blacked out, because when I finally blink back to reality, my hands are around Candy's throat, and I'm straddling her naked body on the bed, her pink fingernails clawing at my forearms.

My eyes widen in shock, my hands instantly falling away from her delicate throat, as she gasps for breath, tears leaking from the corner of her eyes.

"Please," she gasps, her hands wrapping around her chest protectively. "Don't hurt me. Please. Let me go, and I won't tell anyone."

It would be meaningless if she were to die from strangulation.

That's too easy, and not what I want. What I need is for her to bleed for me. I need the ultimate sacrifice to calm me down and clear my foggy mind.

"I'm sorry, Candy. You never should've gotten in my car." Placing one hand around her throat, I keep her pinned against the bed, while my other hand reaches across to the nightstand, grabbing the black pen sitting on top of the white notepad.

Her body shakes with uncontrolled sobs underneath me. "I want you to know I'm sorry. I hadn't planned on the night ending up like this. I wanted to fuck you, but this is your fault." Tracing the tip of the pen along her frightened face, I offer a smile as I stare down at her fearful image. "You have the wrong shade of blue eyes." I move my left hand up to her mouth and cover it, and without hesitation, I raise my right hand that holds the pen and bring it forcefully down to her throat, piercing her tan skin with the plastic item.

The sound of her muffled screams tickles the palm of my hand, her body shaking underneath me. My eyes remain locked on her frightened blue orbs as I remove the pen, blood pouring out of the wound in her skin, and bring it down repeatedly, piercing her beautiful skin over and over again with a fucking pen.

Her throat is a mangled mess by the time I gain enough control to stop myself.

Still straddling her body, I drop the pen to the floor and adjust myself so her breasts are barely visible beneath me. The sight of the beautiful crimson liquid flowing out of her punctured skin has my cock standing at painful attention between my legs. Swiping my hand along her throat to collect her blood, I wrap my hand around my length, stroking it and tugging a few times to completely cover myself, using her blood as my lube. My balls tighten at the first stroke, my eyes fixated on the sight of my blood covered cock and her gurgled sounds.

"Fuck," I rasp, my bicep flexing while I set a steady rhythm, stroking myself furiously, chasing the release I desperately need. Keeping the pace, I use my left hand and shove two fingers into one of the wounds on her neck, chills shooting down my spine at the feeling of the soft warm tissue of her neck. The sight of me practically fingering her throat has me ready to paint her blue lips in cum, but I refrain. I remove my fingers, reaching behind me, and then I shove them into her pussy.

"Holy fuck." My eyes roll back in my head at the feel of her walls snug around my fingers. Both my hands work in perfect rhythm, the left thrusting in and out of her pussy while the right jerks my cock, my grip around my shaft nice and firm.

"Fuck, fuck, fuck, oh fuck," I chant, my stomach tightening, warmth settling at the bottom of my spine as I explode, thick white ropes of cum spraying from my head and landing on Candy's neck and parted lips.

Gasping for air, I roll off her, lying beside her rapidly cooling body. My chest heaves as a smile spreads across my lips. A metallic smell lingers in the air; the scent alone is enough to get my cock to come back to life despite just having reached a release.

Turning my head to the side, I look at the dead woman beside me.

She didn't deserve this, but it's not my fault. When I picked her up, my intentions were pure. I planned on losing my virginity tonight, but something in me changed the moment we got behind the locked door and I stared into her blue eyes.

I snapped, and everything after that was beyond my control.

She's not the one I wanted. She's not Lee. Everything about her was wrong, and now her blue eyes that were the wrong shade are lifeless.

It wasn't my fault.

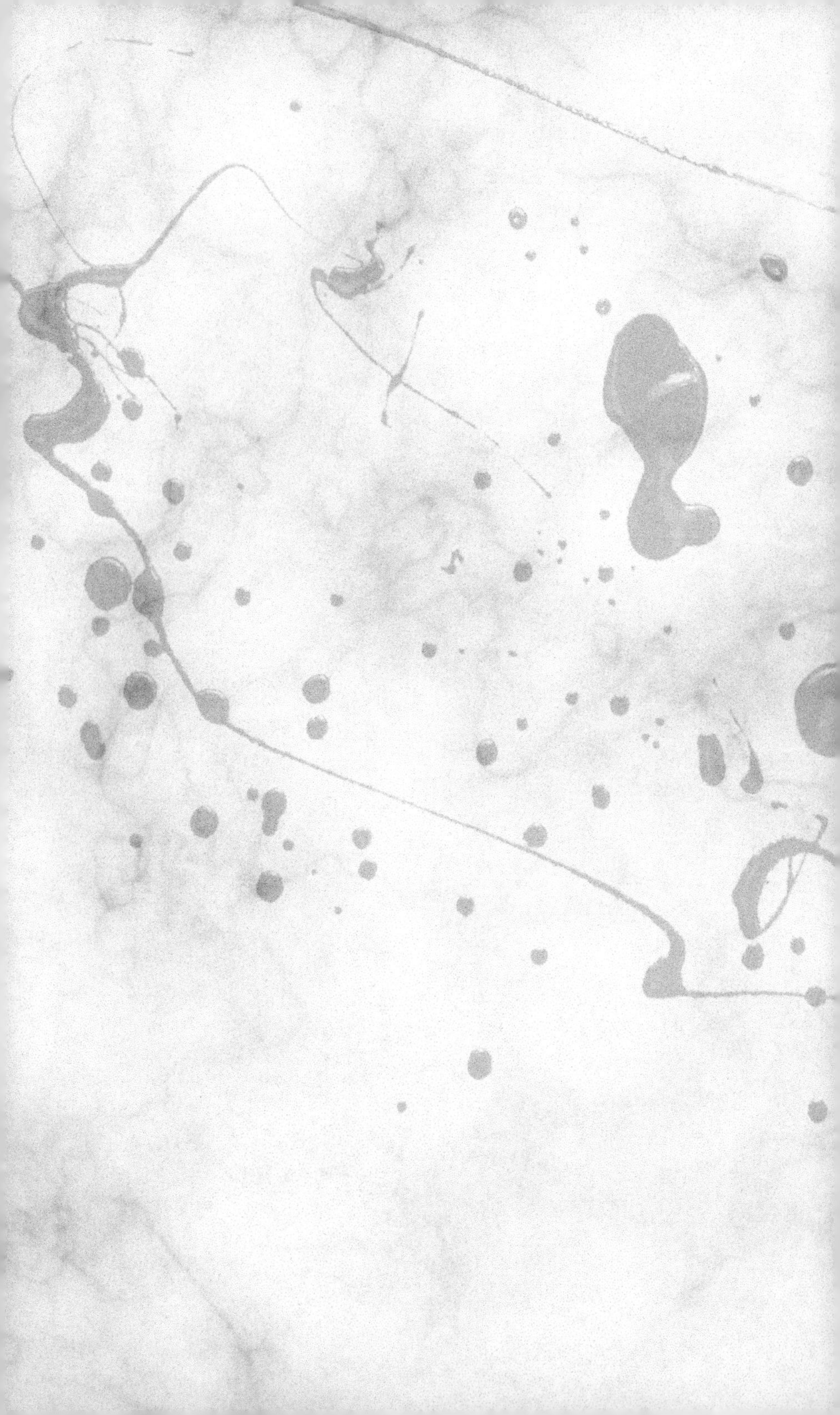

Chapter Eight

TWENTY-FIVE YEARS OLD

My pretty thing got married yesterday. On my birthday, of all days. I wonder if she thinks of me or even remembered that yesterday was my birthday.

It's been years since we've spoken, although I see her nearly every day.

Her smile was wide, and her dress was fucking ugly and unlike anything I ever thought she'd wear.

It wasn't the white dress I imagined her wearing when she'd walk to me, vowing herself to me for eternity. But this is her first marriage after all, so it didn't matter what she wore or who she's marrying, because one day, it'll be me.

Her perfectly posh husband doesn't realize what a perfect jewel he married. Nor does he realize what a gracious man I am. I could've easily snapped his fucking fingers for touching what's mine, or better yet, snapped his neck, but I didn't. I haven't touched a single hair on his blond head.

Trust me, I've had many chances and have been very tempted.

I could've easily run him over when I followed him home one day while he was out for a run. It would've been an accident. I didn't, though, because my pretty thing thinks she loves him. Bless her little heart for being so damn confused.

She's pretending to be someone she's not. I helped her do it. Thanks to me, she has a clean background and could tell her uptight husband whatever story she wanted to about her background.

Lee didn't want to be that little girl from foster care anymore. She wanted a new life, so I gave it to her. There's nothing too big or too small that she could ever ask me for. I'll give her anything.

She could ask for my heart, and I'd rip it out of my chest and serve it to her on a silver platter with my dying breath.

Lee needs to get certain things out of her system before it's time for us to be together. We will be reunited even if it's not today or tomorrow.

One day.

Against my better judgment, I attended their wedding.

Lee and Sebastian.

She didn't know I was there because I've gotten pretty good about sticking to the shadows, but I was there, watching her exchange vows with someone she met a few months ago.

She's known me for twelve years and still doesn't see what's right in front of her. All these years and she still hasn't realized that we belong together. She's clearly a little slower than what I give her credit for, but I'm willing to wait because it needs to be her decision.

She needs more time to realize I'm the one she belongs to.

I never said I liked her decisions or agreed with any of them, but she more than earned the right to make mistakes. I wouldn't be able to protect her from everything, and if I tried, she'd fight against me because that's who she is.

Which is why I haven't pushed us into being together yet.

Despite me being ready for her, she's not ready for me.

I had sat back in the corner of the reception venue, eating the stuffed chicken that I wanted to hate, and watched as the seemingly happy couple shared their first dance. I felt like my cover was blown a few times and she might have seen me, but I always slipped away when she looked toward the corner where I was sitting, and her ocean eyes would end up on an empty chair.

Like I said, I'm pretty good at hiding in the shadows.

That's what happens from years of staying silent and being forced into the background to avoid being abused.

Father and my foster parents have taught me valuable lessons.

Like how to lie underneath someone's bed without them ever having any idea.

I'd been so desperate to be close to her I snuck into their hotel room on their wedding night to see what lingerie she planned to wear for him.

I'd been so caught up sniffing the red thong on the bathroom floor I lost track of how long I'd been in the room, and before I knew it, the newlyweds were rushing into the room, and I had no choice but to slip underneath the bed.

Not my proudest moment.

The first time I heard Lee come, I had wanted it to be for me, not for someone else, but thanks to losing track of time, that didn't happen.

While Sebastian fucked her into the mattress, I fucked my fist with her red thong wrapped around my face so I could smell her while I imagined what it would be like when her hot cunt slid down onto my cock for the first time.

When she came, I came, using her panties to catch the biggest load I'd ever spilled.

I waited under their bed until their breathing deepened, then with the wet panties in my hand, I slipped out from underneath the bed, shoved the dirty thong into her mouth, cum and all, then slipped away into the stillness of the night.

I wish I could be there in person when she wakes up in the morning with her panties in her mouth along with a mouthful of my cum, but I'm not willing to risk being caught any more than I already have. Watching via camera will have to do.

Luckily for me, after leaving their room, I didn't have to go very far; I rented the room right next to their suite. I'd hoped the rooms would have adjacent doors, but that didn't happen. It's fine, because all it took was watching and waiting until a housekeeper turned her back on her cleaning cart, leaving her master key unattended. I'd swiped it yesterday when I walked past, and that's how I let myself into their room.

This morning, I lie in the middle of the king size bed, holding my phone in front of my face as I watch the screen, watching my pretty thing from the view of the camera that I set up in their bedroom.

Her golden hair is spread across the pillow as she sleeps peacefully, her naked body covered by the white sheets. The spot next to her is empty, thank fuck, but I can hear Sebastian's annoying as fuck voice coming from somewhere. If I had more time, I would've been able to place cameras in each room of their suite, but thanks to being distracted by her dirty panties, I was only able to place one, placing it above the mounted TV in their bedroom.

She looks like a fucking angel lying there. Someone too perfect for me. If I were a good man, I'd leave her alone instead of dragging her into the depths of hell with me, but we've already established that I'm not a good man.

Pinching the screen, I zoom in as close as I can get, laughter unexpectedly erupting from my lips at the sight of the red thong poking out from her parted lips. Part of me expected her to wake up during the night as some point after feeling the fabric in her mouth, but to my delight, she didn't. Lee has always slept like the dead. Even during our time together in foster care, nothing could wake her until her body was ready.

Her shoulders move as she coughs, her brows furrowing as her eyes flutter open, confusion taking her.

Lee coughs, one hand clutching the sheets tighter against her bare body while the other hand comes up to her face. Her fingers reach inside her mouth, and she slowly pulls out the red material.

"What the fuck?" she mumbles, licking her lips. She looks at the material in disgust, tossing it to the side of the room. Her delicate throat bobs as she swallows, licking her lips repeatedly.

I know she can taste me. The scowl on her face is all the confirmation I need.

Good, that's all I wanted to see.

Swallow it all, baby, because soon you'll be swallowing me regularly.

One of these days, she'll be on her knees begging me to fill her up, and I'll have only one question.

Which hole?

Clicking off the camera app, I lock my phone, kick the sheets off, and sit up. I know from reading Sebastian's emails that he plans on taking her on a honeymoon to Italy for two weeks.

Lee deserves to see the world, but I should be the one taking her, which is why I cancelled their reservations and deleted the cancellation confirmation emails from his account. They'll arrive at the airport tomorrow, ready to board their flight, only to discover they've cancelled it.

Sure, he could book another flight and another hotel, and of course I thought of that. So, to make sure they wouldn't be going anywhere, I hacked into his scheduling system at work and put him on the schedule.

He'd blocked time off for the two of them, but thanks to me, he's back on the schedule with upcoming surgeries, as well as being on call. I should feel bad because my pretty thing doesn't deserve that, but one day when I tell her everything I've ever done for her, she'll understand. It's for her. Everything is always for her.

I walk into the bathroom and remove my boxers before stepping inside the walk-in shower. Twisting the knob, cold water falls down on me from the rainfall showerhead in the ceiling. I adjust the temperature, getting it to the perfect setting, then wrap my fist around my cock and stroke it until I'm shooting cum down the drain, replaying the image of my pretty thing's face when she woke to discover panties and cum inside her mouth.

Once I'm out of the shower, dried and dressed in one of the fluffy hotel robes, I order room service, selecting nearly everything that's offered on the breakfast menu. I'll have them charge it to Sebastian's room later.

I let him marry my girl. The least he can do is buy me breakfast.

I spend the remainder of my day in the hotel room, rotating between watching the camera in the next room and masturbating. They have the same idea, too, because most of the day I watch Sebastian and Lee in bed, wishing like hell it were me in that bed with her.

When they have sex, I turn the volume up and strip out of the robe. I should turn it off and give them privacy, but I want to hear every noise that my pretty thing will make. I don't watch the screen, but I do set my phone on the nightstand, smiling when the sound of Lee's moans fills their room and mine.

"Hold on, pretty thing. Wait for me," I whisper to no one, bouncing across the room to my duffle bag. Digging around, I find the clear bottle I'm looking for and return to the bed, spraying the pillows and blankets with the perfume.

It's Lee's favorite scent—Vanilla Diorama. Ever since I gifted her a bottle of it on her eighteenth birthday, she has been wearing it religiously. When I smelt it at the mall one day, I knew it would be perfect for her, so I stuck a bottle in my pocket and walked out. I couldn't afford it then, but I can now. Except, I stole it from her vanity the day I broke into her house.

The vanilla scent along with the sound coming from my speaker allows me to pretend she's here with me instead of being separated by a wall.

Climbing on the bed and lying down, I bend my left hand and place it behind my head and use my right hand to wrap around my aching cock, using the dripping beads of pre-cum to lube myself up.

Had I been smart, I would've stolen a pair of her panties while I was in her room. That's okay; I'll raid her hamper for a dirty pair when I go to their house. Maybe if I'm lucky, I'll even be able to steal those tight spandex shorts she loves to workout in.

God, I'm practically salivating at the scent.

My imagination, along with the smell of the perfume, is enough to make me come, ropes of cum shooting from my cock onto my abs and chest. I keep stroking, squeezing the tip until I've completely milked myself and the moaning coming from my phone has ended.

Licking my fingers clean, I turn to look at the screen, ignoring the man next to my woman.

"Don't worry, baby. We'll be reunited soon."

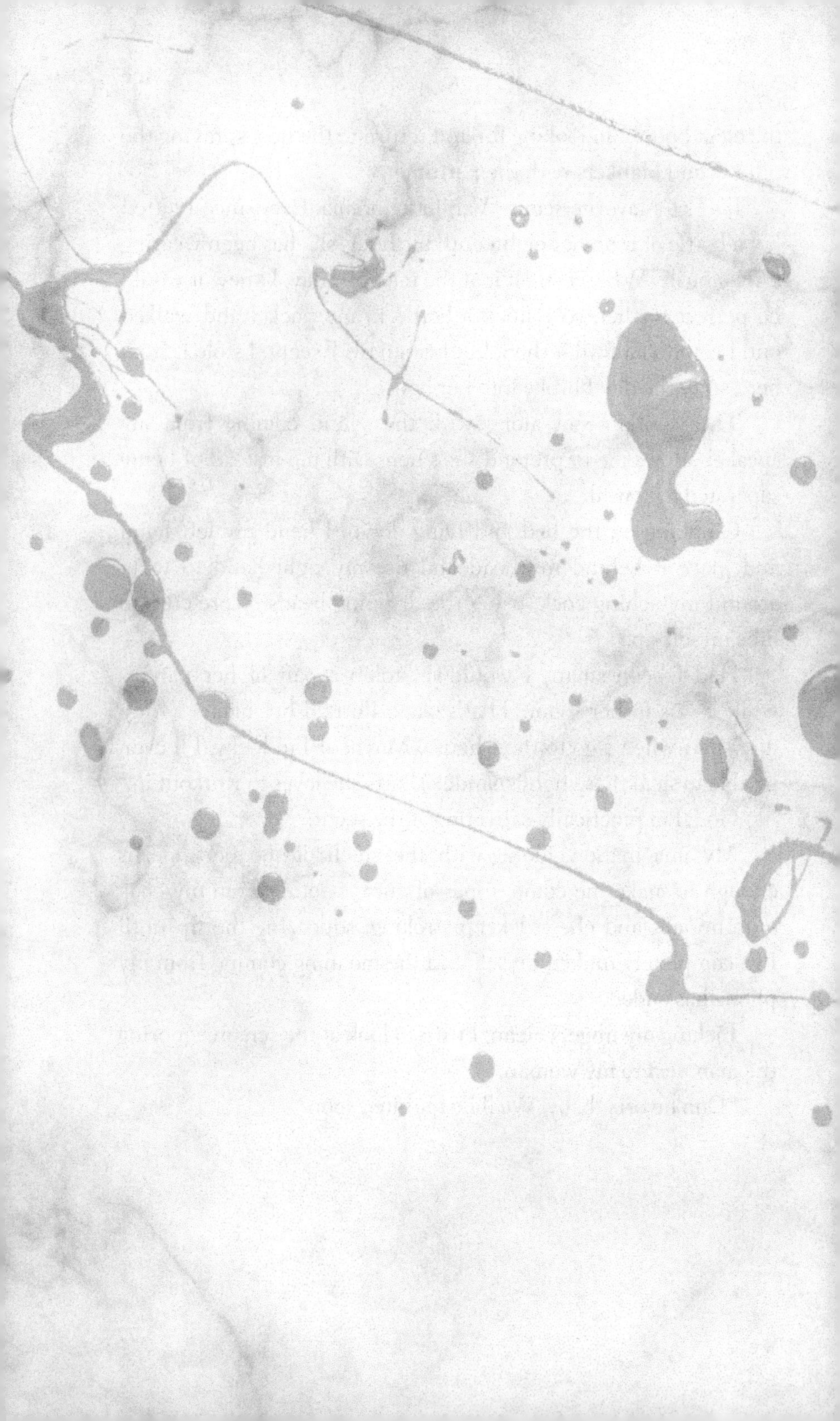

Chapter Nine

TWENTY-SIX YEARS OLD

KILLING IS EASIER ONCE YOU GET THE FIRST FEW OUT OF the way. For me, it took three to feel comfortable doing it. By my sixth victim, things had changed. In the moment, I told myself it was a coincidence they all had blonde hair and blue eyes, but after claiming the life of a sixth woman, I realized I did indeed have a type.

I was using women as a surrogate for her. Doing to them what I wanted to do to her.

No, I don't want Lee dead, but I want to watch her bleed. Punish her for making me wait and everything else she's put me through over the years. I want her to bleed for me, the same way my heart constantly bleeds for her. The women I've killed temporarily patch a void in me that only she can fill.

It's been a year since she married Sebastian, and much to my dismay, they're still together. They have the perfect fucking life while I'm still hiding in the bushes outside their house, waiting for any glimpse of her I can get.

They have everything.

They've got money. A nice house. Nice cars. Great careers.

Well, my pretty thing doesn't have a great career anymore. She's no longer dancing. She's teaching instead. It drives me crazy that I don't know the reason for that drastic change. She's always loved dancing, but she gave it up out of the fucking blue.

The less I know, the angrier I become with her, and the longer we're apart, the stronger the urge becomes for me to claim another life. I can stop. I know I can. The second she comes back to me; I'll stop because I'll have her. The real thing.

If only she knew the deaths she's responsible for and will continue to be responsible for.

All it would take is for my pretty thing to return by my side. For her, I can be better. I can learn to let go of the devil that has had his claws in me since I was a child.

Today is my twenty-sixth birthday, and to celebrate, I began my day with hunting. I'd found the perfect blonde-haired blue-eyed vision this morning, and she went willingly to a motel with me, just like they always did. All it took was the promise of cash for her to jump in my car and whisper sweet nothings in my ear while I drove to the same motel, taking her into the same room I had killed the first whore in.

Candy.

After I'd slit her throat and coated my skin in her blood like it was some part of a spiritual ritual, I touched my cock until I came all over her blue lips. The sight was so fucking ethereal, I couldn't stop myself from becoming hard again, forcing her mouth open, and fucking it until I came in her pretty little dead mouth.

My cum had gathered in a pool at the back of her throat, the sight making me go feral as I realized it would be there forever. She'll decompose and eventually become nothing but bone while my cum lingers, day by day fading away along with her flesh.

I marked her forever.

I had been the last thing she'd seen as she took her final breath. Meanwhile, she was simply another body to pass the time, another name on my growing list of victims. You'd think that the women meant nothing to be, but you'd be wrong. They meant everything.

They were my therapy. Their blood was cleansing my soul, helping me to one day rid myself of the devil that lived inside me.

After I was finished taking a two-hour long shower there in the motel, I'd cleaned up the scene. To make sure that not a single drop of blood could be found, I scrubbed the room thoroughly. I'd learned to prep the room before bringing the whores there, so after Candy, I started using a plastic sheet to protect the mattress from their blood seeping into the foam. I didn't want there to be any trace of them.

I'd gathered the body and bloody blanket into the back of my trunk, then disposed of her in a trash field four hours outside of town. Her last resting place is with bags of trash, where she'll never have a chance of being found. Seemed fitting.

I never use the same field twice. Can't risk having their spirits plot against me, so I keep the women separated.

Right after returning home, I took another shower and got myself ready for my dinner reservations. Thanks to my unlimited access to Sebastian's emails, I'd found where he planned to take Lee tonight for their one-year anniversary and made myself a reservation. This is as much my day as it is theirs.

That's where I am now, sitting at my table in the corner of the dimly lit restaurant, with a clear view of Lee from where I sit.

Her back faces me, her blonde hair hanging perfectly straight down her back, not a single strand out of place. An awful pink dress covers her body, the sleeves long, and the hemline even longer. She looks like a Barbie doll that escaped the box. The sight makes me want to laugh, but I refrain because even though she looks fake and unlike the girl I remember, she's still the most beautiful woman I've ever seen. It doesn't matter what she's wearing, because underneath it, I know she's still that girl that doesn't mind getting down and dirty.

Lee may look like the perfect suburban wife, but I know her deepest, darkest secrets, and that's something that her perfectly posh husband can never say. He'll never know her how I do.

He may know the fake made up life stories she's told him while she pretends to love him, but I know her true heart. I know the monsters that lurk behind those blue eyes, and the secrets she'll never allow leave her lips.

This phase of her life is temporary. One day, she'll come to realize that.

"Sir, are you ready to order?" The redheaded waitress interrupts my staring. Blinking, I turn my attention to the girl who doesn't even appear to be old enough to drink.

"I'll take the toffee caramel cheesecake, then afterward, I'd like the ribeye steak with garlic fries. Medium rare." Snapping the menu shut, I hold it out toward her.

"So, you'd like the dessert first? Before your meal?" she questions, her thick eyebrows scrunching together in confusion.

"I like my dessert first," I explain, keeping my answer simple. I could tell her that since I've been on my own, I prefer eating dessert before dinner, because I have an insatiable sweet tooth and too many times in my life, I've been denied of something sweet. As a child, my mother would often make my favorite dessert, chocolate cake with a homemade whipped cream and caramel frosting that she'd top with pieces of butterfingers and toffee bits. When I was good, she'd allow me to help her make it. I'd always lick the spoon when she wasn't looking or dip my fingers in the mixing bowl.

I'd wait all day for a piece of cake, only to be denied by Father after I'd finish eating my dinner. To make it worse, he'd force me to sit at the table and watch him eat the biggest piece of cake. My mouth would salivate, watching him savor every bite. So, I vowed to myself that I will never be denied such a simple pleasure again once I have money of my own.

Besides, I know that one of these days my sins will catch up to me, and if my life is going to end, I'd rather it ends after I've fed my sweet tooth. Then I can truly die a lucky man.

"Yes, sir, I'll get your order placed and bring your cheesecake right away." The waitress takes my menu before scurrying off, her red hair disappearing from my sight.

The sound of sweet, feminine laughter fills my ears, and my eyes zone in on the sight of Lee as she brushes her hair from her shoulders. She reaches a hand across the table and grabs hold of Sebastian's open palm that's reaching out for her.

Their lips move, but I can't hear what they're saying over the other voices in the room. I can only hear Lee's loud laugh. She pulls her hand away, and I hold my breath as I watch as her head turns over her shoulder, her eyes scanning over the occupied room of patrons dining.

For a moment, I hope her turquoise eyes will land on me, but they don't. Instead, she leans into her husband and says something that makes him nod. She scoots her chair back, stands, and follows the signs toward the restrooms until I can no longer see her.

My palms grow sweaty and goosebumps break out on my skin as I sit there, feeling more alone than ever. My mismatched eyes scan the dining floor, hoping to see her, but she hasn't yet returned.

Standing from my chair, I choose to follow my pretty thing, hoping for another glimpse of her. I'm not sure why, when I'm already at risk of her seeing me, but I enjoy putting myself at risk.

Walking through the doors of the dining room, I walk along the white painted hallway, one foot in front of the other until I get closer to the restrooms where only a door will separate me from my love.

Turning the corner, I stop in my tracks, gasping at the sight of the woman in pink.

Lee leans against the wall, her pink heeled foot tapping while she crosses her arms over her chest, emphasizing the cleavage peeking from the sweetheart neckline of her dress.

"Ace. I thought that was you I had seen in there." Her eyebrows are pulled together in a scowl, her eyes thin slits as she stares at me.

"Hey pretty thing, did you miss me?" I smirk, shoving my hands in my pockets.

Her eyes narrow at me, a huff leaving her parted lips.

Oh shit. She's fucking furious, but I will not lie and say that seeing her angry isn't getting my dick hard.

"What the fuck are you doing here?" she whisper-shouts, her eyes widening and looking over my shoulder as if she's expecting to see someone else there with us.

"What do you mean, what am I doing here? Last I checked, this is a restaurant, and I'm here to eat."

She eyes me slowly from head to toe, her arms falling to her sides as she straightens her posture. "No, you're not."

A smirk tugs at my lips. "No? What am I doing here, then?" Removing one hand from my pocket, I reach out and brush a piece of silky blonde hair behind her ear, tugging on the diamond earring in her lobe.

Her breathing halts, her eyes softening at my touch. For a moment I hope that she'll jump in my arms and tell me she's ready for me, instead she steps back, creating a distance between us. "You're following me." Her voice is a breathy whisper, and I can practically hear how fast her heart is beating.

Closing the gap between us, I trail my fingertips along her delicate heart-shaped face, my eyes drinking in the sight of her.

Touching her feels so fucking surreal, and if I'm not careful, I'll come in my pants like an immature boy. Nothing compares to the feel of her soft skin beneath my fingertips.

"So what if I am? What are you going to do about it, pretty thing?"

"Don't call me that." Her whispered words fan across my lips, her body trembling under my touch.

"Why? You're my pretty thing. You always will be, even if you have another man's ring on your finger."

"Ace, please."

"Please, what, baby?"

Her blue eyes look from my lips to my mismatched eyes. Her perfect eyes betray everything she's feeling. Lust. Anger. Remorse. Confusion.

Leaning down toward her, my forehead rests against hers, my large, tattooed hands gripping her small waist. "Stop thinking so much, just say yes."

"Say yes to what?"

"Say yes to being mine. We both know we're inevitable, and you've been playing games for far too long."

She's silent for a moment. Hope builds inside of me but dies as quick as it grew at the sound of her sigh. "I'm married, Ace."

"Do you think I care about that bastard out there? He doesn't know shit about you."

Her slim fingers push against my chest, forcing the distance between us. "He's my husband, and I love him." Her mouth says one thing, meanwhile her eyes say another.

"Who are you trying to convince? Me or you?" My teeth clench, my jaw hardening. "Do you still love me?"

She avoids my gaze, looking everywhere but at me. That's all the confirmation I need. She may be afraid to admit it, but little does she know her reaction to the question betrays her.

She fucking loves me, which means there's still hope for us, but she's not ready yet.

"Don't worry, baby. I don't mind waiting, as long as you don't keep me waiting too much longer." I've been waiting fourteen years already. What's a little more time?

"Ace." Her shoulders sag in defeat. "Leave me alone. Please, just leave me the fuck alone and let me be happy."

Laughter rips free from my parted lips. "Happy? You really think that the fucking tool sitting at that table can make you happy?"

"I made my choice when I asked you to help me remove myself from my past. I need to move on, and you're not letting me. Please, if you love me, you'll leave me alone."

"That's your problem, pretty thing. You like putting Band-Aids on bleeding wounds, hoping it'll solve your problems."

"What's it going to take for you to let go and let me forget my past?"

"Nothing! I love you, so I'll never let you forget it. You pretend it doesn't exist, and that's never going to help you heal. You refuse to acknowledge the shit you've been through, and that's why you'll forever be that damaged nine-year-old girl."

Her eyes become glossy with unshed tears. "Fuck you, Ace! You are my past, and Sebastian is my future. You—" Her words fade on her tongue, and the second I wrap my ink-covered fingers around her delicate throat, her eyes widen.

I growl my words in her face. "He may be your fucking present, but don't for a second think I'm not your future." Releasing her neck, I shove her away from me.

"I already have your past, baby. And I've been kind enough to share the present, but I will claim your future. Get that through your thick fucking skull." A smirk tugs at my lips, "Or I can fuck it through your head if you prefer." The tears she's been fighting to hold back release, the drops running down her face, leaving black streaks of mascara.

"Please, Ace, please. Let me go. Just leave me alone," she begs in defeat, tears falling from her sad eyes, reminding me of a cloudy sky and light rain.

Placing my thumb on her lips, I apply pressure and swipe, smearing her glossy pink lipstick across her face. "Next time I see you, you better fucking be ready. I will not be so willing to walk away again."

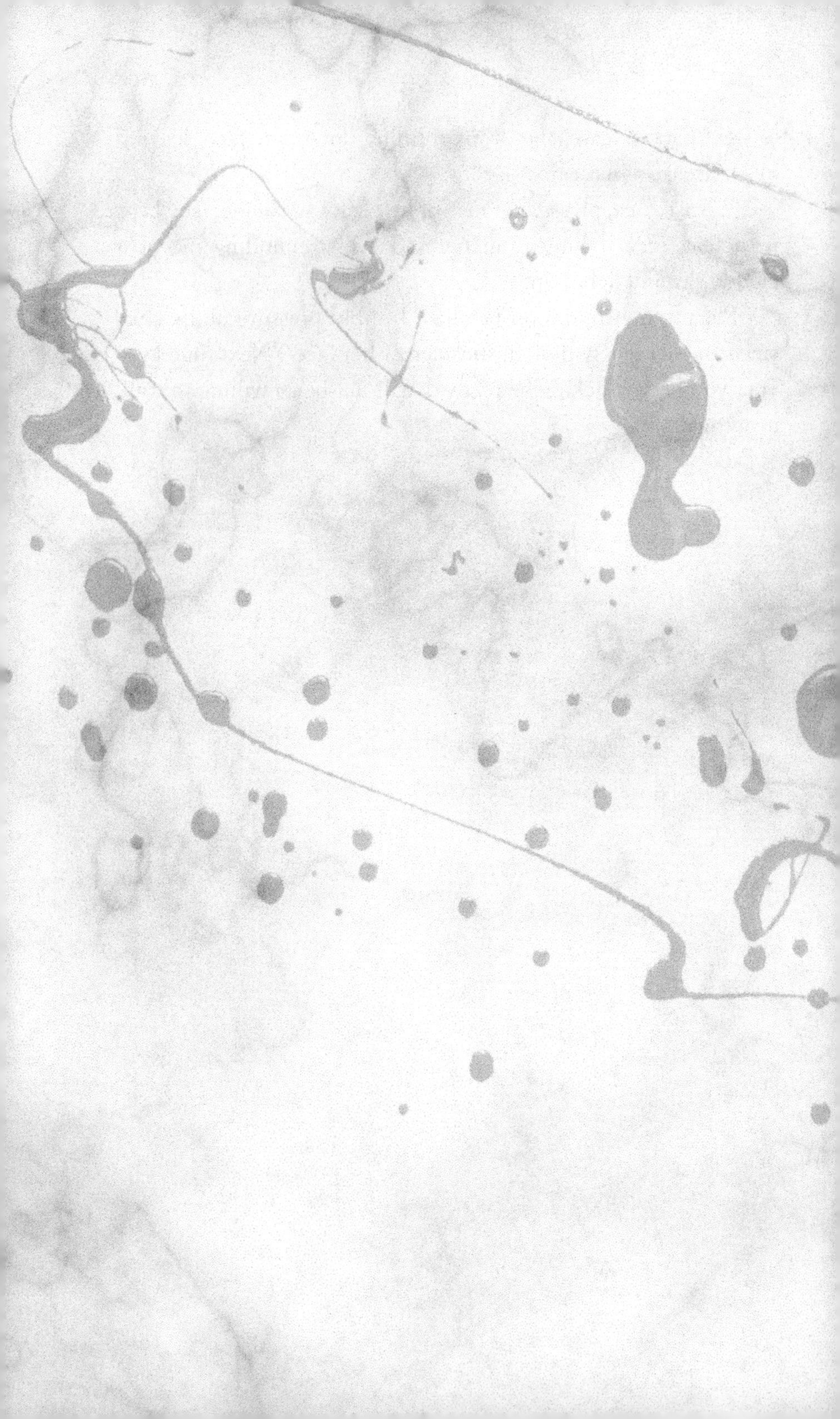

Chapter Ten

TWENTY-NINE YEARS OLD

It was a cold Tuesday at the beginning of fall when my phone rang. The screen had lit up with an image of my golden-haired beauty. The photo was one I'd taken from afar while she'd been out grocery shopping. She'd smiled at the young worker who bagged her groceries, and I pretended it was me she was smiling at when I captured the photo from where I hid behind a shelf. That day, I set the photo as her contact photo, and for the last few years, I've been waiting for my phone to light up and showcase that photo.

Call me pathetic, but I'm a man with an unhealthy obsession. A lovesick fool, waiting for the day my lost girl finds her way home to me.

When Lee asked for space that day at the restaurant, I granted her request. As much as it made me physically ill to be apart from her, I quit following her. Stopped tracking the GPS in her car and cell phone, stopped reading their emails, stopped following her every movement. Instead of fawning over her, I worked on improving my computer skills and stacking my cash, getting everything in place for the moment she returned to me.

I spent countless hours on the dark web, chatting with other hackers who could help me grow my knowledge of codes. Even I can admit when I need help. Thanks to my friends online, I grew my skills to the point I could become wholly untraceable online and could hack into any system should I choose to.

It's amazing, the things you can learn online, hidden away in the dark web. Anything your heart desires is one chat or click away. After all, that's how I learned. While watching my mother on the computer for years, I took every chance to learn useful skills whenever I could use it.

After my mother died, it was my online friends that helped me to expand my knowledge. They were the ones who helped me become the hacker I am today and would often wire me money to help me out once they knew I was homeless after running away from my last foster home.

Because of my newfound skills, I could help my pretty thing all those years ago when she came to me, asking me to cover up her past so she'd be able to live a normal life. Little did I know, by doing that, it would allow her to marry that Sebastian fucker.

Regardless, it's because of my skills that led me to the phone call that I'd been waiting for. I hadn't wanted to seem too eager, so I waited four rings before answering, practically coming in my pants at the sound of Lee's throaty voice in my ear.

My heart swelled with hope, wishing she were calling to say she wanted me. Instead, she was calling because she needed a favor. Again.

Her request had left me shocked. "Help me fake my death." That was the first thing she'd said to me when I answered the phone. The call lasted forty-six seconds, and by the end, we set a date to meet.

She'd told me she had a plan but couldn't yet tell me. She

requested a new identity, already having a name in mind. The urgency and desperation in her voice had me agreeing, no questions asked. She said we had to meet some place she often went to because her husband would track her.

We meet at her hair salon with the paperwork for her new identity in my hands. Seeing her again after not having a single glimpse for years just about gave me a heart attack. The sight of her was everything I'd been imagining in my head while I'd spent countless nights fucking my fist.

Three minutes was all the time she granted me. She wore black sunglasses that were too large for her face, but I could see the dark bruises peeking out from underneath the shades, regardless of how much she tried to hide it. She had a black eye but refused to tell me anything more.

All she said was, "If you love me, you'll give me the new identity and let me go. I promise to call when it's safe." That was enough to make me turn over the documents, allowing her to continue with her mystery plan and new identity.

The moment she drove away, I went home and concocted a plan of my own.

That was seven months ago.

She still hasn't called, but Lee isn't as mysterious as she thinks she is. The minute the new name she wanted left her lips, I knew precisely where she planned to go.

Back home.

She was leaving Sebastian and going back to the city where all her demons live.

It's both poetic and therapeutic as fuck, if you ask me.

Knowing where she'd choose to go, I followed my pretty thing. Not only are her demons here in the city, but so are mine.

Being here meant it was only a matter of time until he discovered she was back.

Rowen...

The only other foster brother apart from me she loved, and who loved her in return.

She broke their promise to never return, and because of that, I inserted myself into his life. Which was easy to do, considering we'd never met.

Rowen isn't aware of what I, Ace, look like, but I know all about him. I've made it a habit to learn everything possible about the men my stubborn pretty thing loves. Rowen being one of them.

Despite telling her to leave the city, he never did. He stayed, starting Hale Enterprises with Eli and King. Two men he refers to as his brothers.

It was easier than expected to insert myself into his life, especially when a job posting opened up at their company. I wish I could say it was luck that they were looking for a new IT tech, but I may have had something to do with the previous tech needing to leave the company abruptly.

No, I didn't kill him. But I may have made an anonymous call informing him he was the lucky raffle winner at his local grocery store and needed to come in immediately to collect his million-dollar winnings. It's not my fault the naïve sucker quit his job right away and raced downtown to the grocery store hosting the raffle.

That part wasn't a lie. There was a raffle, but I'm certain the prize was a free, reusable shopping bag.

What kind of idiot believes a store would give away millions of dollars?

Idiot.

Hopefully, he picked up a job application while he was there.

You know what they say. One man's loss is another man's gain.

Truth is, I didn't want to work here for Eli, King, and Rowen.

Waking up every morning, putting on my best attire, and sitting at a desk surrounded by idiots telling me what to do isn't my idea of fun.

The things I fucking do for my girl.

She came back here, and knowing Rowen the way I do, I know it'll only be a matter of time until he finds her. When he does, I need to be informed immediately, which is why I'm here, sitting at a desk with a nameplate that says *Travis*. My alias.

Rowen may not know my face, but he knows my name, and I couldn't risk him connecting the dots. I'll be here as long as needed to keep my pretty thing safe.

Until I'm certain Rowen isn't a threat.

"Hey, Travis." Eli steals my attention away from the computer screen I've been staring at for the past thirty minutes while lost in thought. "Can you do something for me?" He sits on the edge of my desk, and his dark eyes study me as if he's uncertain about what he wants to ask me.

Since the day I began working for them, I've been trying to earn their respect, hoping to become one of the trusted people in their inner circle. So far, it's been seven months, and I've yet to be welcomed in or hear anything about Lee from their mouths. I know she's here, but instead of going to her, I choose to remain working where I am, watching Rowen's every move.

However, if they don't trust me soon, I may have to say fuck it and get my pretty thing my damn self and get the fuck out of town. Perhaps I'll take her away to an island and keep her chained to the bed, forcing her to remain with me.

The thought causes a sly grin to spread across my lips, but I remember Eli is here. "Sure. What can I do for you?" Underneath the desk, I cross my fingers, saying a silent prayer that he'll trust me to do something important.

"This needs to stay between us. You can't run to Rowen or King about this. Can I trust you?"

I wipe my sweaty palms on my pants, biting my bottom lip to hide the anxious grin threatening to make an appearance. I've been waiting for one of them to trust me and let me in. "Absolutely. Anything you need, I'm your guy."

"Good to know." He pauses, looking over his shoulder to make sure we're alone. "There's a new dancer at Sinners. She's someone from Rowen's past that seems to knock him off balance. He's becoming obsessed, and I'm worried it's going to interfere with our business."

While he speaks, I do my best to keep calm, hiding the excitement I feel knowing that he's talking about Lee.

"How can I be of service?"

"Monitor both of them. If he tries to go near her, I want to know right away. Access the tracker on his phone if you need to. I want to be informed if he so much as *thinks* about that girl."

Nodding, I let my hidden grin break free and spread across my face. "You got it, boss. You'll be the first to know."

"Good. I'll be in touch if I need anything else." Eli stands, turns his back to me, and walks away. He leaves me sitting there with the world's biggest grin.

Fucking finally.

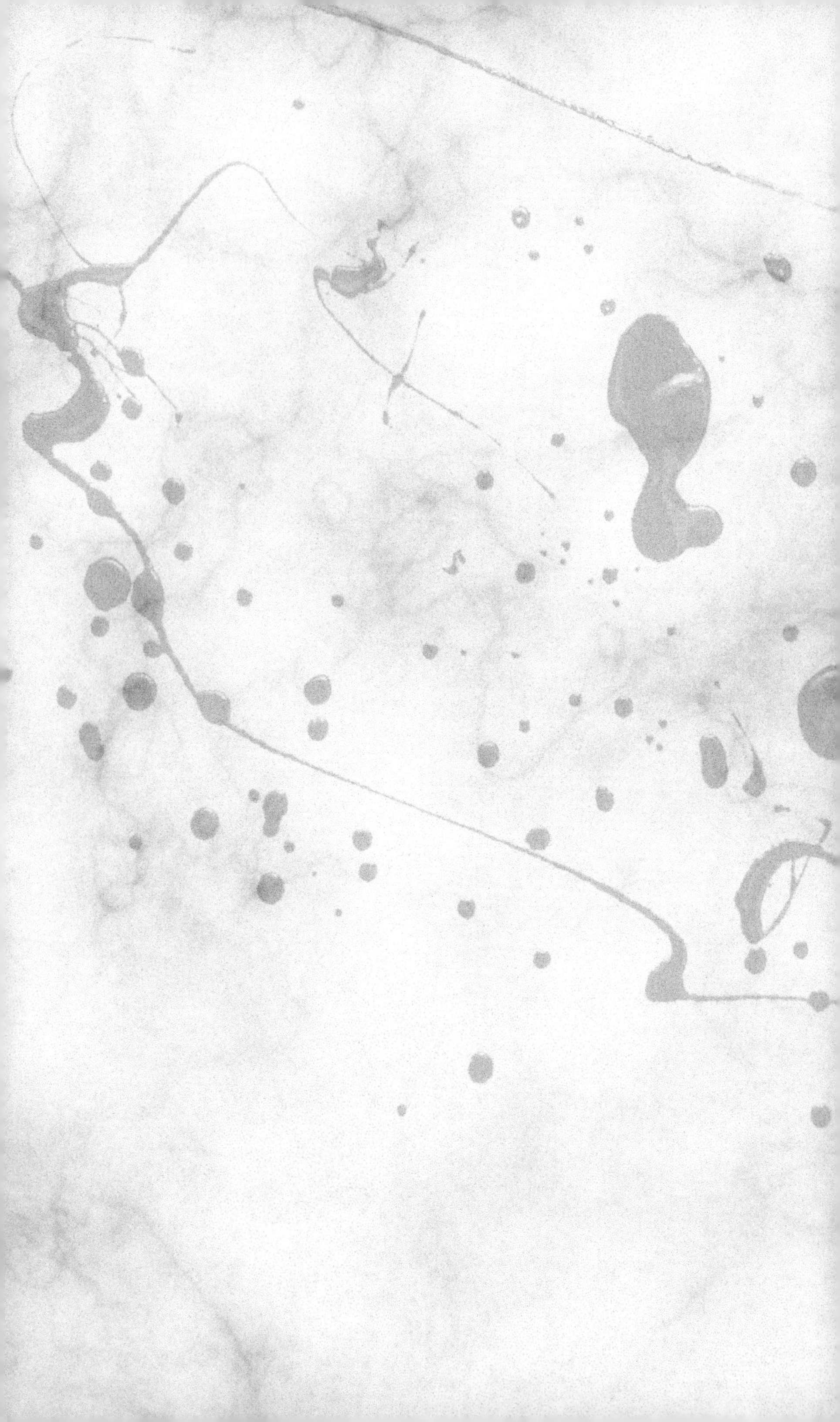

Chapter Eleven

THIRTY YEARS OLD

My patience has run out.

I've watched my pretty thing go from being married to one man, to jumping into a weird relationship, if you can even call it that, with three men.

At this point, I don't care if I have to kidnap her and lock her in a room until Stockholm Syndrome kicks in. I've been more patient than any other man would be, and it's time for her to be where she belongs once and for all.

With me.

I've waited and left her alone like she asked me to that day I helped her obtain a new identity to run from Sebastian. Although, I should've killed that fucker, but she begged me not to. As much as she hated him, and killing him would've been easy, she wanted to see him get arrested for her faked murder. Lee wanted to have the last laugh while he was forced to sit in a cell for the rest of his life.

While I was left with my dick in my hand, trying to remain

hopeful that she'd come back to me, she was busy pretending to be someone new, yet again.

Instead of being with me, she was alone, which resulted in getting herself kidnapped; the past always has a way of coming back to bite you in the ass when you least expect it.

It's ironic. She wanted to forget her past so badly, but the monster that once lurked underneath her bed found her and wanted his pound of flesh.

Since leaving Sebastian, Lee's actions have been so fucking stupid.

It's a good thing I've been watching after her, because who knows what the fuck would've happened if she'd been truly on her own.

Six months ago, I started cleaning up my act to prepare for our reunion. I've learned to control my urges and haven't claimed a life since.

I wish I could give all the credit to my obsession with my pretty thing, but I can't.

Annie, my last victim, was partially the reason I stopped killing. She'd fought back more than all the women before her combined. The first punch had taken me by surprise, but I ultimately subdued her and slit her throat.

Two weeks later, I'd seen her photo in the newspaper. She was a twenty-three-year-old mother, and when she didn't come home from work that night, her mother reported her missing.

Annie wasn't like the other women. No one missed them, but there were people out there missing Annie—people who would never get answers as to what happened to her.

Seeing her in the newspaper triggered something within me and made me realize I can't continue on the path I was going down.

One day I want to have a daughter, just like Annie. How will I be able to look my child in the eyes after the things I've done?

How will I ever be able to hold my child in my hands after I've used my hands to claim so many lives?

I threw up every day for a week, and for the first time in many years, I got down on my knees and prayed. Even went to church every Sunday, hoping that whatever God was in the sky listening to me would take mercy on me, relieve me of my demonic urges, help me repent for my sins, and allow me to have happiness.

I set up an anonymous trust fund for Annie's daughter and paid off her mother's house. She'll never have to worry about making the monthly mortgage payment. Once the girl turns eighteen, she'll have unlimited access to the funds, and she'll be able to afford whatever college she attends—if she goes. Regardless, she's taken care of for the rest of her life.

Money can't make up for the fact her mother will never be there to watch her graduate or get married, and that's something I'll regret for the rest of my life. I fucked up.

I'm fucked up.

I made a horrible mistake that I regret daily.

The only thing I can do now is continue to pray that God continues to show mercy and doesn't change his mind.

If my pretty thing knew the monster murderer I'd become, she'd never want me. That in combination with the regret from killing Annie is what kicked my ass into gear. I'm still looking for a new hobby, but I can guarantee my next hobby will be completely legal.

I may be pathetic, but I've still been holding onto hope that we'll be together in the end.

Just the two of us.

Forever.

And tonight, it looks like I'm going to get exactly what I want once and for all. I'm going to get the girl, and once I have my hands on her, I'll never let her go.

I've been tracking Lee since the moment she was taken from

the back alley at Confess. I've been tracking and waiting, watching from the background, waiting for my chance to come out of the shadows and claim my girl.

Following her led me here, to the red brick house where she's being held captive. I was prepared to rush in moments ago, but as expected, Eli, King, and Rowen arrived, ready to rescue my pretty thing.

Instead of rushing in, I remained across the street, watching from the darkness as the three of them charged into the house, ready to rescue the damsel in distress.

That was twenty minutes ago, and now I'm growing tired of waiting.

Placing one silent, booted foot in front of the other, I sneak across the street, heading toward the back of the house. I let myself in and observe that the house is quiet, but I know they're here.

They're taking too long, and I'm not sure why, but this only goes to show that they're unable to protect her the way I can.

Perhaps they need a little incentive.

With a smile on my face, I remove the small bottle of lighter fluid that I'd placed in my waistband. Then, I squirt the liquid over everything in the living room.

Taking quiet, careful steps, I continue squeezing the bottle of fluid around the surfaces in the outdated house, using every drop of liquid.

Setting the empty bottle on the counter, I remove the pack of matches from my pocket and spark one to life, watching the flame dance around on the stick in my fingertips.

I've held life in my hand many times. I've been the one to choose between life and death, and it's never felt as good as this moment. I know that my pretty thing is in this house, but even with setting the house on fire, I know she'll make it out.

Either they'll save her, or I will.

Regardless, she'll be safe.

I'm willing to risk everyone else.

Dropping the match, the liquid instantly ignites in flames, the bright warmth spreading quickly across the floor, engulfing the curtains and sofa in a wild glow of orange and yellow.

Covering my mouth and nose, I run out of the house, returning to my safe zone across the street.

It doesn't take long for Eli and King to rush out of the house—or for Rowen to meet them outside. The sight of their empty hands has me balling my hands in fists, fuming at the fact they left the most important person to me inside the burning house.

Selfish fucks.

They'd rather save themselves than the girl they claim to love.

Once they leave, I slip back inside the house, the smoke instantly burning my lungs and nostrils, my eyes watering and skin beginning to sweat from the heat.

Fire is unpredictable, but it's no match for a man who has already lost everything he once loved and is refusing to lose another person.

Eli, King, and Rowen let her down. They let *me* down.

Instead of risking their lives, they left her behind, fucking chained to a wall in the basement.

They left her alone and bleeding, apparently not giving a fuck if she died there.

Fuck. Them.

This further proves that I'm the only savior she needs in her life. I don't think twice about running into the basement, freeing her from the chain around her ankle, and rescuing her from the flames that threaten to claim her as a casualty.

I risk myself because that's what you do for those you love; besides, it was a test, and they failed. If I weren't willing to run into the fire to save her, I never would've set it. I only hoped that they would've been the ones to save her.

Especially Rowen.

With my girl in my arms, I run us the fuck out of the burning house, sucking in gulps of fresh night air.

The flames baptize me, absolving me of my sins. This was God's test for me. Walk through fire to be cleansed from every wrongdoing.

For her, I'm willing to walk through the flames of hell. I'd burn alive if it meant saving her, and now I have the chance to make her see that.

I have her back, and this time, I will never let her go.

She won't escape me again.

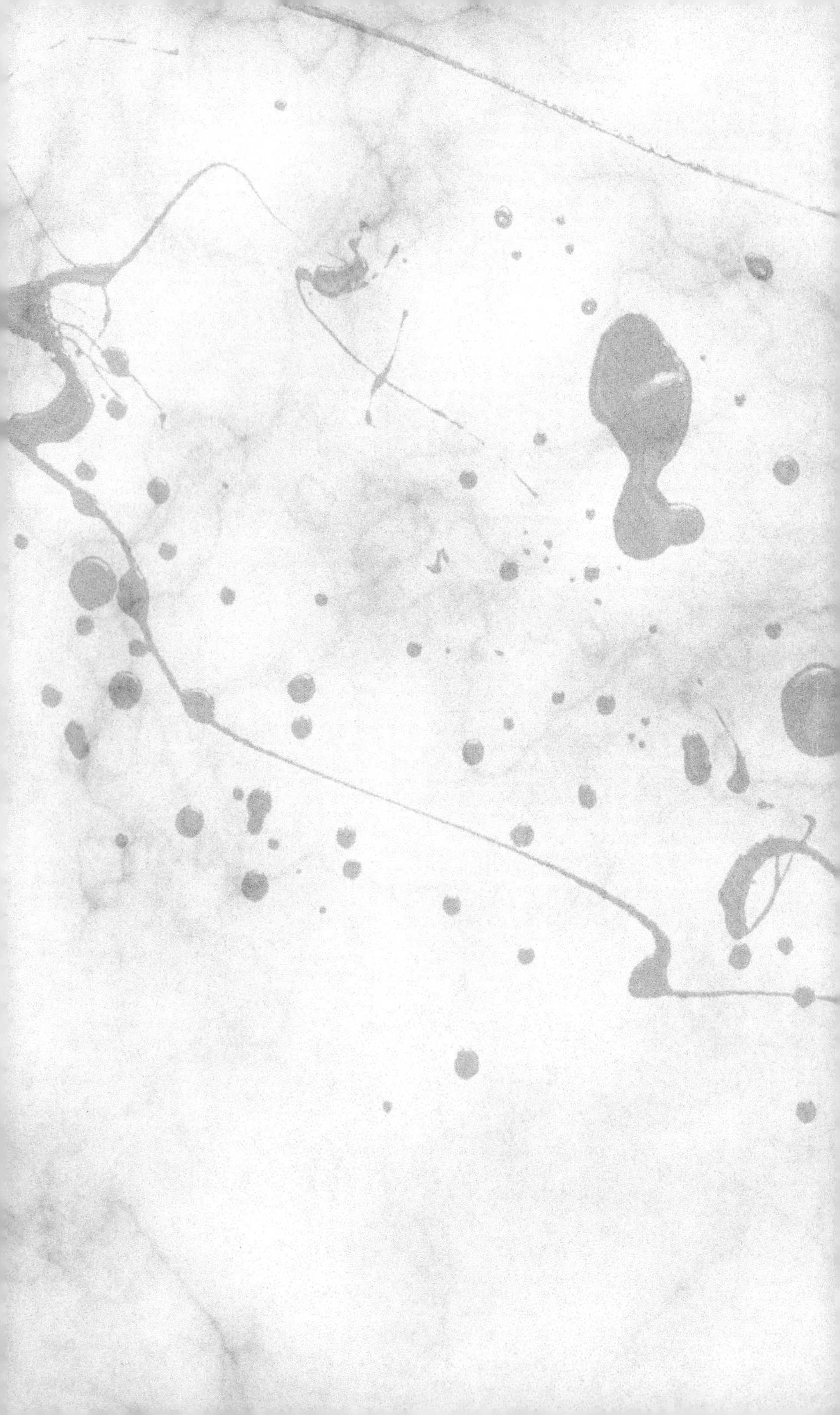

Chapter Twelve

THIRTY-ONE YEARS OLD

It's been two weeks since the night that will be remembered as the night that forever changed multiple lives.

One week since I wore the light blue suit I'd bought specifically for the occasion.

I'll never wear it again.

One week since I held my pretty thing in my arms while she sobbed uncontrollably, begging us to end her suffering. When we declined her request, she threw herself at the blue casket and said that we should bury her with him if we loved her.

With Eli.

Today marks one week since his funeral, and two weeks since he's been gone.

Two weeks since his rare laughter filled the walls of our home.

Two weeks since I've heard his voice and seen the shit-eating grin he'd always try to hide.

Eli was a complicated man with walls so high it sometimes

felt impossible to get through them. It took a lot of effort to get to know him, and often I felt I still didn't actually know the complicated man that was Eli Michael Hale.

One thing I know for sure is he loved deeply. He loved his brothers, and he loved our daughter.

Most of all, he loved her.

Although he tried to deny it, I know he loved me, too. Eli loved me when I didn't love myself or know how to love anyone else besides her. He taught me a lot during the time I spent with him.

I've never bothered telling Lee, King, or Rowen about the times I spent with Eli because they felt too personal to share. They don't need to know that every Thursday he'd lie about working just to take me to visit my mother's grave where we'd spend hours. Sometimes we'd talk. I'd share pieces of my childhood, and he'd share pieces of his. Other times, we'd sip our coffee and sit in silence.

Every single Thursday, without fail, Eli would be by my side at the cemetery. When I needed to cry because I held onto so much anger toward my mother, he'd be my shoulder to cry on. When I needed to get my anger out physically, he'd be my punching bag.

When I needed to lose myself in ecstasy to mute the voices inside my head, he'd oblige. However I needed him, he was there.

That's the thing about Eli.

He was always fucking there. For anyone. Whenever, wherever.

Now, he's gone.

He's gone, and there's an endless pain in my chest. I can't sleep because he consumes my dreams.

Lee's a ghost. She doesn't eat, drink, speak, and she doesn't see me. She blinks, but stares right through me. King had to physically force her to take a shower, and as soon as she was clean, she dug Eli's clothes out of the hamper and put them on. She used to fight us, but she's given up altogether.

Being home feels haunted. I hate being there. Hate having to walk past the spot where Eli died. It kills me a little more inside each time. The silence is too much. None of us know how to act, and except for Lee, we're doing the best we can for the sake of Olivia. Our daughter needs someone strong enough to be there for her to have a shoulder to cry on, which is why King, Ro, and I have been taking shifts to care for her.

Sometimes it's too hard, because I can't stop myself from expecting Eli to walk through the door at any moment.

The feeling of losing someone you're in love with is a pain I'd never wish on anyone. I'd give anything to never feel this way again. If I could've traded my life for him, I would've.

This morning I managed to fall asleep on the couch just as the sun came up and filled the living room with rays of orange, red, and yellow. I slept for a few hours until I woke to the bitter aroma of coffee.

The house was quiet, the coffee pot was off and hadn't been freshly used. The phantom scent of coffee reminded me of Eli, which is why I left without saying anything. I needed to be near him, because he needs to know how fucking angry I am.

That's how I ended up here. At the cemetery on a chilly Saturday morning, sitting in the grass that's wet from the morning mist of sprinklers, the cold earth soaking into the fabric of my sweatpants. I don't mind, though. I'll take any feeling I can get. I've been numb for two weeks.

Even with paying expedited fees, Eli's headstone will not be ready for at least another month. For now, he's stuck with a small temporary metal memorial marker. It doesn't feel real, being here and seeing his last resting place, knowing his body is six feet below me.

A chuckle slips past my lips. "That was pretty damn selfish of you, dying on me like that. You know, if you didn't want to continue our weekly cemetery therapy sessions, there were other ways to get out of it." A smirk spreads across my lips. If he were sitting next to me right now, he'd roll his eyes and call me a smartass, all while trying and failing to hide his grin.

"Why did you leave us, Eli? You were supposed to be invincible, and the strongest. Yet, you gave up. Why didn't you fight back?" My only response is a breeze rolling by, ruffling the blades of grass.

Lee told us what happened the night he died. I can't wrap my head around the fact he didn't try harder to fight back. She explained he didn't try harder to fight back because it would have put her life in danger. There are so many things he could've done differently to change the outcome, but none of that matters now, because he's gone and there's no bringing him back. No matter how badly I wish I could.

Feet shuffling in the distance steals my attention away from Eli's metal marker, my head looking over my shoulder behind me to see two unexpected guests.

"Thought we'd find you here," Rowen says, carrying two Starbucks cups of hot coffee in his hands. King carries an iced coffee, sipping from the straw. The sight is enough to turn my frown upside down.

Lee got him hooked on iced coffee a few months back, and now, no matter the weather, he has his iced coffee in hand daily.

As soon as they reach me, they both sit beside me, and Ro hands me one cup.

"Thanks." I wrap my hands around the cup, hoping the warmth will warm my icy fingers. I should've brought a jacket before coming, but I was in too much of a rush that I came in only sweatpants and a T-shirt. The cold winter air hadn't been on my mind until now.

"What are you guys doing here?" I ask to no one in particular as I bring the cup to my mouth and take a drink of the still-hot liquid.

King clears his throat, his eyes misty as he looks ahead at Eli's name etched into the metal grave marker. "We saw you were gone and knew you'd be here."

"Yeah, we figured we could all use some time away from the house," Rowen says.

Nodding, I allow silence to fall upon us, each of us having our own moment and internal battle.

Finally, I ask, "Where's Liv? Did you leave her home with Lee?"

"Fuck, no," King says. "Lee wouldn't even notice her if she were there." I see the look of sadness that crosses over his and Rowen's face. We all know that Lee is incapable of taking care of our daughter right now. She's too deep into her grief to be present to anything going on around her. "She's having a playdate with Riot for the weekend. Mel came and picked her up earlier." Melanie's family has been a godsend ever since Olivia came to live with us. Parenting is fucking hard, and it really takes a village.

Rowen sets his coffee cup in the grass before wrapping an arm across my shoulders. "We all miss him, Ace. The only way to get through this is if we stick together. We need each other now more than ever before."

"It doesn't feel real. I don't want it to be real. How can he just be... gone?" The first tear rolls down my cheek. "We never should've left the house without him that night."

"Quit thinking that way, Ace." King says with a sigh. "There was no way to know what was going to happen."

His words go in one ear and out the other. "It's our fault he's gone. All of us became too fucking comfortable and stopped looking over our shoulders."

"Is that how you want to live? In fear. Always looking over

your shoulder?" Rowen shakes his head and says, "My fucking heart is broken. My best friend, my brother, is gone. But I know it's not my fault. I've spent years blaming myself for things I couldn't control, and I will not do that anymore. None of us are to blame."

"Then who the fuck is? Eli? Is it his fault he died?" My fingertips dig into the wet earth, my hands balling into fists around the grass and dirt. "I thought I was angry at him, but I'm not. I'm angry at myself for not being there for him."

King lays his head on my shoulder. "I'm angry, too, Ace. But Eli wouldn't want us blaming ourselves. If he could see us right now, he'd kick our asses and call us pussies."

We share a laugh. "Yeah, he would have our heads if he could see this," Rowen agrees.

Inhaling, I admit something I've never allowed myself to say out loud, "You know, I never wanted this. This weird fucking relationship. I didn't want it." I exhale, biting down on my tongue in anticipation of their response.

King is the first to respond. "What the fuck are you talking about?"

Removing my dirt covered fingers from the ground, I wave my hands between the three of us. "This! Lee is the one who wanted it, not me. All I wanted was her and wanting her led me to be with three other guys."

"You don't get her without us!" King snaps, his hazel eyes narrowing. "We want you. I want you. So, what the fuck are you saying?"

"No one is holding you hostage, Ace. If you want to leave, then leave," Rowen adds bitterly with a huff, removing his arm from around me.

"No! There is no leaving!" King shouts, standing to his feet. "We lost Eli, and now you're saying we're losing you, too?"

"No!" I stand, rubbing my hands against each other to remove the dirt. "That's not what I'm saying."

"Then what are you saying?" Ro questions, looking up at us from where he remains seated.

"I'm telling you that this isn't what I wanted... at first. In the beginning, when I found out Lee was with the three of you, I had hoped she'd come to her senses, leave you and be with me. Only me." My shoulders slump. "But now, look at our lives together. We share a daughter, and...and..." I pause, sucking my bottom lip between my teeth.

"And what, Ace?" Rowen finally stands, brushing off the grass and dirt from his pants.

"And now, I love you dumb fuckers!" I admit, surprising them and myself. Saying those three words isn't something that's easy for me. "I'm in love with you guys, and regardless of how I felt at first, now I want this. I want a future with both of you and our girl. This weird family is exactly what I want, now and forever."

A grin spreads across Ro's lips. "Good choice."

King smirks. "Prove it."

"How?" I ask, unease coming over me by the mischievous look on his face.

"Let's get married." He shrugs, as if he just said the most natural thing.

"I agree," Rowen pipes in. "Let's get married."

"Okay, but when we ask Lee, let's not tell her we decided on our future without her."

"Fuck that. I'm not asking her, I'm telling her." King turns his back, walking back to where they parked their car.

Rowen calls out after him, "Where are you going?"

"To get a ring! Are you coming or what?!" With a laugh, Rowen and I say our goodbyes to Eli, then rush after King, ready to purchase rings and take a step to forever.

Eli should be here, and I know in spirit he is.

He will forever be the first man I've ever been in love with.

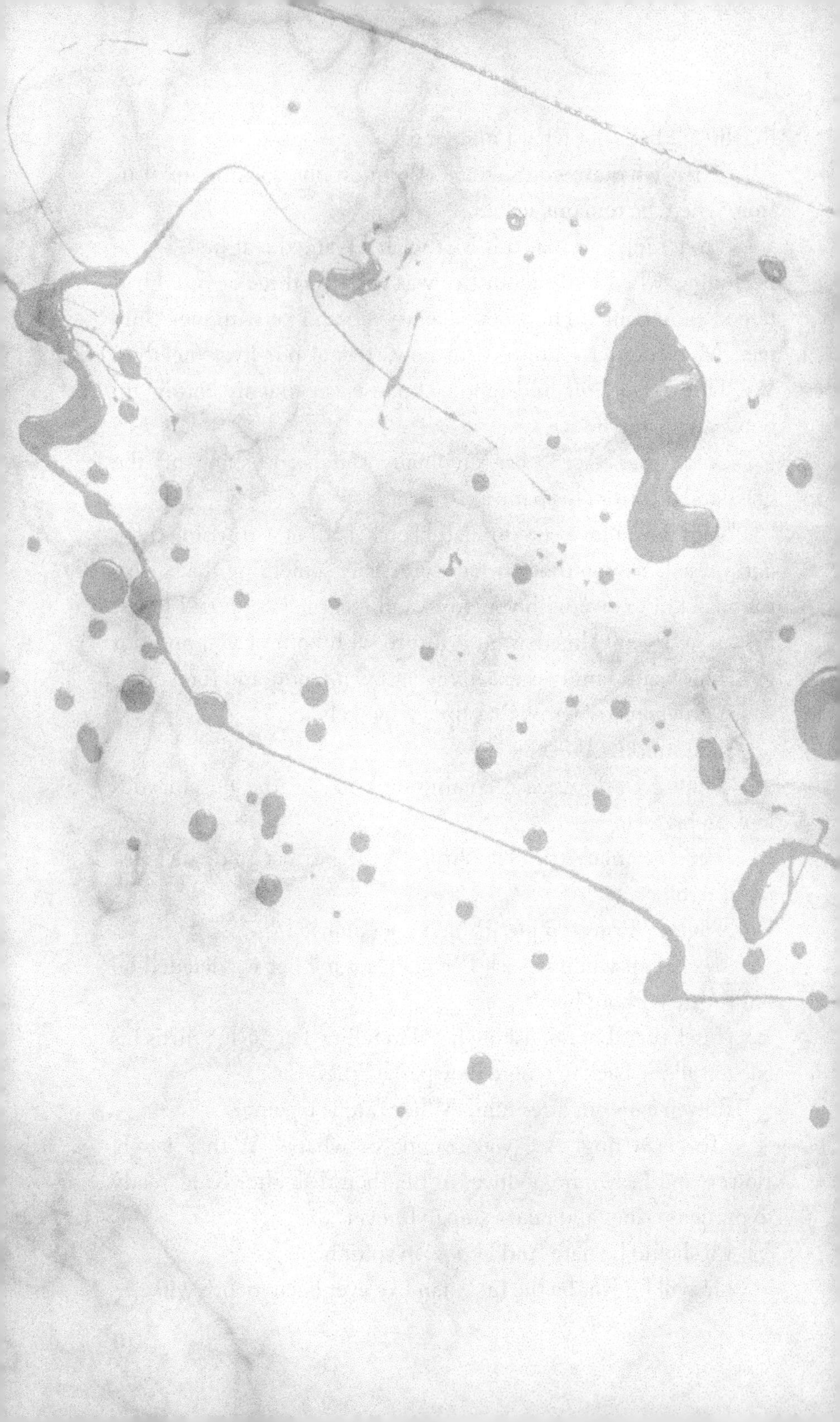

Chapter Thirteen

THIRTY-TWO YEARS OLD

I've been thinking about my father a lot lately.

I've done my best over the years to push him out of my mind, and it took a lot to realize that his punishments were wrong, and I never deserved what he did to me. Not only did he abuse me and betray my trust, but so did my mother.

Coming to terms with that fact was the hardest pill to swallow. My mother had always been my role model.

As a child, I idolized her, but I realize she was as much of a predator as my father. The only difference was she said she loved me and whispered sweet nothings in my ear while she touched me in ways no mother should ever touch their child.

It took many late night conversations with the one person I least expected to realize how truly fucked up my childhood was. Without him, I never would've been able to work through the shit in my head.

Eli.

He had witnessed my silent struggle soon after our unconventional five-way relationship began. When I wasn't willing to talk and reveal my demons to him, he sat me down and urged me to reveal my innermost thoughts.

That night, he shared secrets with me he had never shared with anyone else. Having him open up to me showed me I wasn't as alone as I had thought I was.

I've felt so fucking alone for the majority of my life. The times that I'd truly needed someone, no one was there for me. All I had to keep me company were the voices in my head.

To this day, I'm still learning that I'm not alone, and I don't have to face my demons alone.

These days, I've been more stressed than ever. Yet again, life is changing, and I know things will happen that I cannot control, but I absolutely fucking hate it. I hate not being in control of shit. And even thinking about it makes me feel like a piece of shit.

Lee is pregnant. We're having a baby. It'll be our second child, and I have no fucking clue to what to do.

I've never had a stable role model in my life. The parents I had were awful and the worst possible examples. My fear is that I'll become like them. Not the abusers that they were. Never that. I'd rather die than ever harm my children, and I'd kill anyone who even thought of hurting my children.

But that doesn't change the fact I worry that one day they'll question if I truly love them. The same way I've always questioned if my father ever loved me. Sometimes, it's difficult for me to show affection.

My pretty thing tells me my feelings are valid, and every parent has similar fears of not being good enough. She has her own fears that she often shares. Lee is an open book. Every thought that pops into her head, or feeling she has, she shares it. Communication is important to her. Considering I've been alone for most of my life, it's often difficult for me. Having someone to share my fears with is all new to me.

She's parenting Olivia now, but she missed out on ten years of her life. This is new to her, too.

A baby is new for all of us.

How much will our dynamic shift?

Our son is going to grow up with three fathers. Is that going to fuck him up?

The unknown is fucking *me* up.

I know that I'm already a father because we have Olivia, and she considers us her dads, but our unborn son is different. It feels as if I'm becoming a father for the first time, and the closer we get to Lee's due date, the more I hear my father's voice.

What would he think about the fact I'm married to a woman that I share with two other men? Trick question. I know what he'd think.

He'd tell me I'm shameful and disgusting and living in sin.

For weeks now, his memory has been haunting me, and because of me, our dynamic is already changing.

Lee is losing her patience with me.

Rowan hates me for upsetting my pretty thing all the time, and King wants to sit around drinking tea and talk about our fucking feelings like we're a couple of high school girls at a slumber party.

I'm the one in the relationship that's ruining things, and it's because of my fears.

Days like this are when I miss Eli the most because he'd know exactly what to do. He was the one who was always calm and in control, keeping his cool whenever one of us needed to fall apart. No matter what the situation was, Eli always knew how to handle it.

The past few days, we've been having the same argument.

Lee worries I will not be involved once the baby is here. She fears that because there's a chance it's not my baby she's carrying that I won't want her anymore. She believes it is Eli's child, but until he's born, we're uncertain.

It's hilarious how she can even form that thought in her pretty little head. We haven't gone through all we have, and I haven't fought for her the way I have only to turn my back when the going gets rough.

It doesn't matter to me whose blood will run through our baby's veins, because it'll be my child regardless. It'll be all of ours.

I know King and Rowen don't care about that either, but they're not the ones causing our wife stress, either.

I'm doing a great job of that all on my own.

This morning, King and Rowen left earlier for work, taking Olivia with them to drop her off at school so Lee and I can "work out our differences," as they said. I've tried, but having a rational conversation with a hormonal woman is like trying to convince a pig to fly.

As soon as I opened my mouth to speak, she bit my head off, accusing me of not loving her and telling me I should pack my shit and go.

No surprise, we fought this morning—we've been arguing practically daily.

I'm not good with my words, and even worse with talking about my feelings. It's uncomfortable, and I don't enjoy being vulnerable. As much as I love my wife, I fucking hate putting myself in a vulnerable position.

I hate the look in her eyes when I try to tell her what's weighing heavy on me, and she gives me that same sympathetic look. I don't want her sympathy, but she doesn't understand that.

No one ever cared how I felt, so having three people care is new to me. Excuse the fuck out of me for not being used to something that I've never had for over thirty years of my life.

I'm at the table, lost in my thoughts, when I hear my pregnant pretty thing waddle into the kitchen. Looking at her, I can already see the annoyance displayed on her beautiful face. "We're having a baby in less than a month. You are aware of that, yes?" She places her hands on her hips, her swollen belly perfectly round and peeking out of her yellow T-shirt.

Someone is ready for round two of the same tiring fight.

Sighing, I remove my feet from the chair in front of me and sit up straight in my seat. "Yes, I'm aware."

"What did I ask you to do today?"

"I don't know, Lee, but I'm sure you're about to tell me."

Fury sparks in her clear blue eyes. "The curtains! I asked you to hang up the curtains in the nursery today!"

"Baby, it's eleven o'clock. I have all day to hang the curtains." I roll my eyes, leaning forward to place my elbows on the table, pinching the bridge of my nose.

She doesn't care about the curtains, nor does she snap at Ro and King the way she's been snapping at me. The only reason she's been chewing my head off lately is because I've been trapped in my head, and that's causing distance and fear. I know it's my fault, but damn.

She sniffles. "Do you still want this? Be honest, I need to know. I'm tired of walking on eggshells around you."

I can't help but scoff because if anyone has been walking on eggshells, it's me.

"Do you think this is funny?" I can hear the sadness in her voice. The tears streaming down her sad face guts me. I never meant for my shit to make her worry. For months, I've been telling her how much I want this, but actions speak louder than words. She hasn't been hearing what I've been saying. She's been jumping to the worst plausible conclusions based on the actions I've shown her, and all I've really done is put more distance between us. I haven't been treating her as someone should treat their lover.

Scooting my chair back, I pat my lap. "Lee, baby, come here."

Wiping her tears with the back of her hand, she comes to me, sitting sideways on my lap so her belly doesn't get in the way.

"Why won't you talk to me anymore? You used to talk to me all the time. Please, I need to know what's going on inside your head."

I nod, wrapping one arm around her back. I use the other to wipe her face. "I want you, our baby, and this family more than fucking anything. I will not leave you guys, and I'm sorry I made you think that." My fingertips slip underneath her shirt and trace circles along the soft skin of her back.

"Then what's going on with you?" Her eyes plead with me for answers.

"I've been thinking about my father a lot lately." She stills, my words taking her by surprise.

"Why?" She scoffs, shaking her head. "What about him?" She hates him for what he did to me, which is completely understandable. I hate him more than I ever thought possible. I'm not sure at which point I stopped loving him and began hating him.

"W-wh..." My voice clogs with emotion, so I take a few breaths before continuing. "What if I become like him? What if I hold our baby and feel nothing and hate him like my father hated me?"

"Ace." She hiccups as tears stream down her face. I never wanted her to know my fears because I didn't want to place that burden on her shoulders. "I promise you that you will never be like your father."

"How can you be sure? You can't promise that."

"Yes, I can."

"How?"

"Because I know you, Ace." She shifts on my lap until she's facing me and wraps her arms around my neck. "You are a good man. One of the best I've ever met." Her lips meet mine briefly, her fingers playing with the short hair at the back of my head. "You are a protector. You protect me, and you will protect our children, too. Please stop doubting yourself. You're not your father."

"You. Are. Good." She kisses me, her body melting against mine the best she can with the size of her stomach. "I need you. We need you to be here and present with us. Please, let go of the past. Your father doesn't belong in our lives."

I've been thinking about him for far too long. He haunts my dreams, and I still feel like that young boy living in the attic, holding my breath and listening for my father's footsteps, hoping not to be punished. "I want to see him," I confess. He still lives in the same house; the only difference is that he's married to Penny now, and they have children together.

Lee pulls back in surprise. "What? Why?"

"Because I want to know why he did what he did to me. I'm a father," I say, explaining what I've been thinking about for a while. My hand goes to her bare belly underneath her shirt, tracing circles over her soft skin. "And I don't understand why he hated me so badly. I'm his flesh and blood, but he fucking hated me. Why? What did I ever do? I need to know because I don't want to end up like him." My body trembles at her touch as she places her small hands on either side of my face, holding me in her delicate hands.

"Nothing, baby. You did nothing wrong. He's an evil man, and men like him don't need a reason. It wasn't your fault."

"Why, Lee? Why did he hate me?" Without permission, tears sting my eyes and fall down my cheeks, only making me even more furious. I fucking hate crying and looking weak, but when I look in my woman's eyes, the blue orbs are free from judgment. They always are.

"No one ever wanted me. I was an innocent little boy. What was his reason for hurting me? Why didn't he love me? What made my mother hurt me?" Furiously, I wipe my tears away, hating the salty flavor that enters my mouth.

"You didn't deserve any of the things that happened to you." Her voice soothes me as her lips press gentle kisses over my face. "Say it, Ace. Say that you didn't deserve it."

Through a sob, I repeat her words, "I didn't deserve it."

"Louder, baby. Believe the words."

"I didn't deserve it."

"Louder."

"I didn't fucking deserve it!" A weight lifts off my shoulders at the words I've never said before.

"Again. Tell me you didn't deserve it, and you'll be nothing like him. Either of them."

"I didn't fucking deserve it! And I will never fucking be like those horrible people."

"Will you always be there for our children and love them unconditionally?" Her lashes are wet with tears, and the tip of her nose is red from crying. In her ocean eyes, I can see her fear.

"Yes!" I keep one arm around her back to keep her steady and place my other hand on her belly. "He's not even born yet, and I love him so fucking much. I will be the best father. I promise you, baby. I promise you, son." Leaning closer to her, I bury my face in her chest, my shoulders shaking with silent sobs.

"I've got you, Ace. I'll always be here for you. Please, just don't shut me out again," she begs, her hands stroking my head and back.

Lifting my head to face her, she wipes away her tears with the back of her hand, then wipes my face clean.

"Promise me you won't shut me out again. It scares me when I don't know what's going on with you."

"I'm sorry, my pretty thing. I promise I'll do better. Just know, I'm not going anywhere."

Leaning into her, I press my lips against hers.

"Fuck me, Ace." Her hands slip between us, her fingers rushing to unfasten my jeans. It's been months since I've had her pussy wrapped around my cock.

Four months, to be exact.

Rowen and King have kept her filled and happy, but God, I've missed this. I've missed her.

Lee stands up long around to free herself of clothing, and I follow suit, yanking off my T-shirt and pulling my jeans and boxers down. Sitting back on the chair, I lean back, taking my hard cock in my hands. I give it a couple of strokes, coating my shaft with pre-cum.

Her beautiful breasts hang heavy and full, her belly perfectly round, light pink stretch marks marring the sides of her hips.

God, my woman is a fucking vision. It's been far too long since I've seen her naked body, and even longer since I've claimed it.

Coming closer to me, she wraps her hand around my cock, lining me up with her wet core as she slowly sinks down, soft moans escaping her parted lips.

Her warm, wet pussy wraps so fucking tight around my cock like the tightest hug.

This is all I need. My pretty thing in my lap, her pussy around me, and her lips on mine. Just the two of us finding our moment of peace in the chaos.

Her hands go to my shoulders, her red almond shaped gel nails digging into my skin, her hips moving against mine as she sets her pace, bouncing on my lap.

"Fuck, you're so perfect." My hands grip her wide hips,

helping her to move on my lap the way she could before pregnancy. "Your pussy is so wet and warm." Her plump pink lips part, heavy breaths and moans slipping free.

Reaching between us, I find her clit instantly and apply pressure, massaging it in a circle. "If it were possible without you dying, I'd slit your throat and fuck you so hard as you bleed on me, allowing me to bathe in your blood. But I love you too much to ever be without you, so I can't. Just know, swimming in your blood is what I want. I want to cover myself in you from head to toe. I can't get close enough to you, or deep enough inside of you." I thrust upward to prove my point, getting as deep as I can, which is still never deep enough.

Half the time I'm inside her, I feel like I need to crawl inside her body because I can never get physically close enough to her. If I could, I'd wear her skin around me like my favorite sweater.

She throws her head back, exposing her delicate throat as she laughs. "You say the sweetest shit." Her laughter causes her soft walls to vibrate around me and I nearly combust at the sensation.

"Anything for you, baby." I take one of her nipples in my mouth, biting and sucking on her sensitive flesh. I know her nipples have been sensitive, but I also know she likes a little pain when she's fucked. She's sadistic like that.

What a match made in hell we are.

"Oh, Ace, I'm going to come." Her body shudders in my lap, her walls tightening around me, which is my sign to increase the tight movements on her hardened clit.

"Come, baby. Drown my cock." Her orgasm rips through her delicate body, leaving her shaking and screaming on my lap.

Holding her down by her hips, I keep her still in my lap while thrusting into her, using her soaked pussy to milk my cock of release. With a roar, I explode inside of her, coating her perfect walls with thick ropes of my cum.

What a beautiful mess she is.

Kissing her perfect tits, I pepper open-mouthed kisses up her neck, gripping her nape and pulling her into me, connecting our lips together. "Good girl. Now, get on your knees and clean me up." Her eyes shine with mischief and the promise of another round.

LATER THAT AFTERNOON, AFTER A BLOW JOB AND GETTING to fuck her a second time, we took a shower together and climbed into bed naked, too exhausted to dress.

My cock claimed the little energy she had for the day, and now she needs rest.

Nothing feels better than lying in bed with the love of my life in my arms, feeling our son's movement as he does who knows what inside his mother's womb.

Lee tilts her head back to look at me, her hand on top of mine that rests on her bare belly. "Do you still want to see your father?"

"I do. You faced your demons and got closure with your tormentor, and I think it's time I do the same." She nods, snuggling closer to my side.

For so long, I thought I was strong enough to not face the man responsible for making the first twelve years of my life hell, but if my pretty thing could face her abuser, then so can I. I don't have to do it alone; I have a family that'll be by my side as I finally close the door to the past. As much as I hate the man, he's partly responsible for who I am.

He didn't care about me then; I know he doesn't now. I'm not looking for a father, I'm looking for answers.

It's my strength that is driving me to wanting to see him. Both my strength and my scars.

My inner twelve-year-old boy needs this.

The best thing he ever could've done for me was give me away. That's the only thing I can thank him for, because if he hadn't, I never would've met my pretty thing. I wouldn't be living the life I am now.

This is something I need to do to focus on healing my trauma.

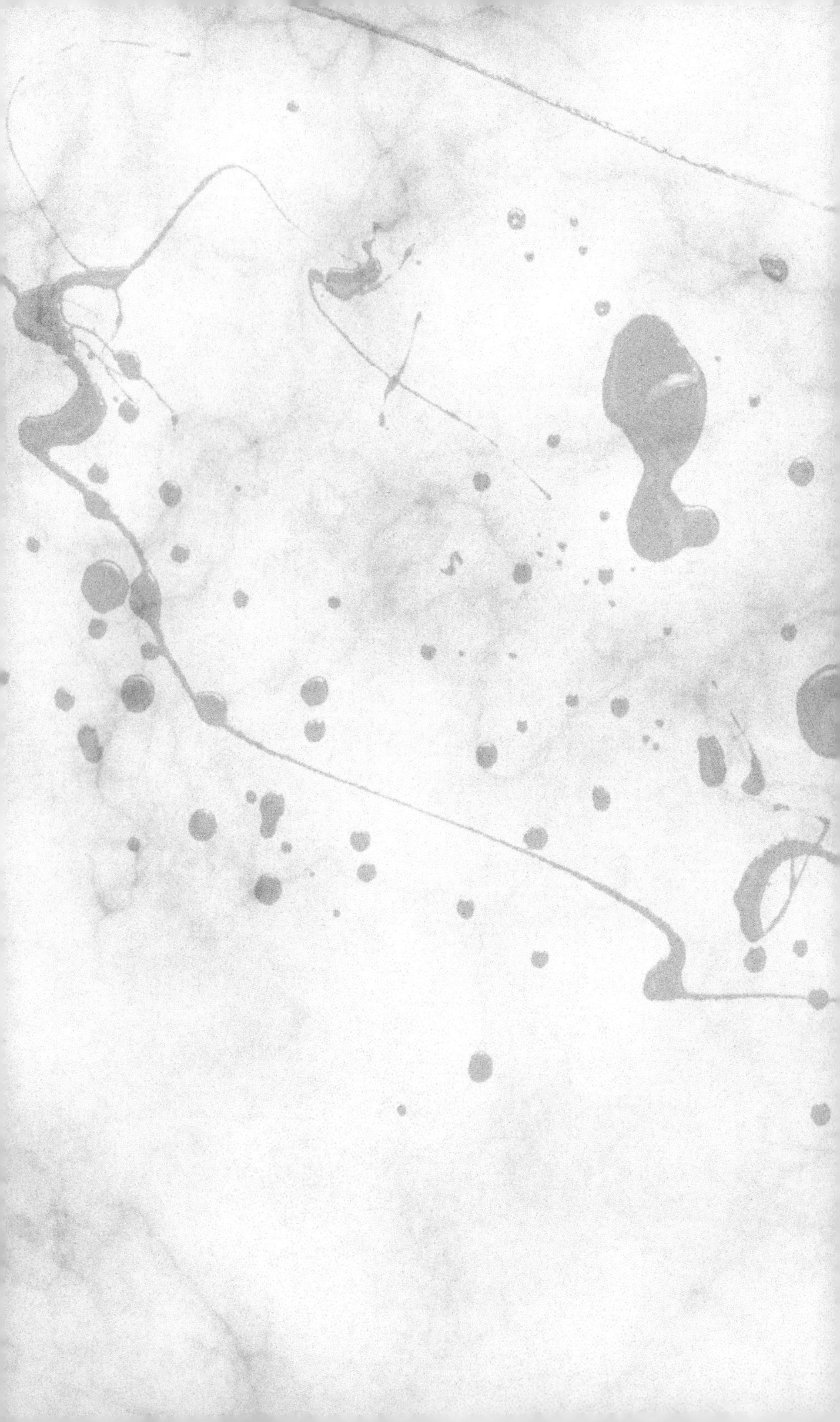

Chapter Fourteen

Today is the day I've been dreading for weeks.

The night I told Lee that I wanted to see my father, she had me sit down with King and Rowen when they arrived home, and together, we broke the news to them, telling them how I needed to face my abuser in order to get closure.

They didn't understand at first, but once Lee explained how she felt better after facing Sebastian, they understood my desires to face my father after all these years.

It was no surprise that they supported me. If there's one thing my family will do, it's support me—no matter what.

Lee wanted to be by my side, but considering she's heavily pregnant, I told her it would be best for her to stay home and rest. Obviously, I'm uncertain how seeing my father again will play out, especially after twenty years, and I don't want my wife caught in the middle. Matter of fact, I don't even want my father to see my wife. He doesn't deserve to see her beautiful face or even know her name.

Which is why I'm going alone.

Back to the house that holds many memories, prepared to

face the monster who's been lurking under my bed for far too long.

I stare at my mismatched eyes in the mirror, my hands nervously straightening out my navy dress shirt, freeing it of the imaginary creases.

When I told my pretty thing that I wanted to dress fancier than normal today, she ironed it for me this morning. Keeping myself well-dressed makes me feel good, not because I want to impress my father. For so many years, I was the kid dressed in too small clothing, with shoes that didn't fit.

When I met Eli, I thought it was ridiculous that he wore a suit every day. I can count on one hand the number of times I saw him wear anything casual. Once I asked him why he was always in a suit, even if he was staying home, and he said it was his armor. Something simple he could do every day to give him confidence and make him feel like he could take on the world.

He compared it to a woman having that one dress that would make them feel like the sexiest woman in the room.

I thought it was ridiculous at the time because Eli was always a confident man. He was cocky and way too fucking confident. It was always something I admired about him.

His confidence, that is.

After tucking the shirt into my matching dress pants, I roll my sleeves up to my elbows, allowing my tattooed forearms to show.

Father will not appreciate the ink that covers my skin, but his opinion of me doesn't matter to me anymore.

After a last glance at myself in the mirror, I exit the bathroom and make my way downstairs in search of my wife, whom I quickly find in the living room on the couch.

"Hi, my lover." Lee's face lights up when she smiles, her blue eyes shining. "You look hot. If I weren't already forty-two months pregnant, I'd suggest you bend me over and put a baby in me." She wiggles her eyebrows.

A chuckle bursts free from my parted lips. "God damn, I love you." I press a kiss to her forehead, then to her belly that she's currently using as a table to hold a Styrofoam to-go box of nachos —her latest craving.

"Talk to me, A. How are you feeling?"

"Surprisingly, I'm okay. I need this, and I'm eager to get it over with."

"If you need me, call me." She sets the takeout box to the side, holding her hands up out toward me. Grabbing hold of her, I pull her up. "I'll be here when you get back for whatever you need. If you need the magic between my legs to make you feel better, then come home and do me," she says, her eyebrows raising when I laugh.

"I'm serious. Even if I'm asleep, roll me on my back and stick it in. If you want to wake me up to get on all fours, I can do that, too." The fact she's serious makes me laugh even harder. Lee has always been a horny little thing, especially while pregnant, but as she's getting closer to her due date, her sexual appetite has become insatiable. She has three men and still can't get enough.

At this point, I'm not sure if she's stockpiling orgasms because she'll have to go without for a while after she gives birth, or if she's just using us to induce labor. Either way, I'm not complaining. Being between her legs is my favorite place to be at.

"Sure, baby, whatever you want." Pressing my lips against hers, I give her a kiss. "I'll be home later. I love you." We share one last kiss before parting ways. She returns to the couch, and I go outside, locking the door and setting the alarm behind me.

Walking down the walkway to where my SUV is parked in the driveway, I stop in my tracks, seeing King and Rowen leaning against it. "Damn, it's about time. We've been waiting out here for you." King pushes away from the car, making his way around to the passenger side.

"You have?" My brows raise. "Why?"

"Do you really think we'd let you go alone? We've got your back for whatever happens," Rowen says, placing his hand on my shoulder once I'm within reach.

"We're family, Ace. You're not doing this alone," King adds.

Emotion clogs my throat, preventing me from speaking, so I nod instead.

"Mel is picking the kids up from school and will come over to keep our missus company. Liv has been begging for another sleepover with Riot." King's mention of our daughter and her best friend cause Rowen to roll his eyes. Olivia and Riot are inseparable, and Rowen hates it. I'm positive that if Riot's parents weren't our best friends, he'd forbid them from spending so much time together.

I climb into the driver's seat, while Rowen grumbles under his breath and gets into the back.

With shaky hands, I drive us toward the house I haven't seen in twenty years.

Three hours later, I'm parked across the street, staring at the faded yellow house with the white door that's haunted my dreams for far too long. My father still lives here. He has another new family.

Sharon died years ago, and my father married Penny, his stepdaughter, the day she turned eighteen. They've been married for fifteen years and have two children. John is seventeen, which proves they were fucking when she was underage. Their youngest, Amy, is ten.

I know what my father is capable of, and after learning he had more children, I always wondered if he was a monster to them like he was to me.

Does he hurt his children the way he hurt me and their mother?

"Do you want us to go to the door with you?" King asks, his hand resting on my shoulder as I stand between him and Rowen.

"No, wait here. I need to do this alone."

King wraps his arms around me, hugging me tight.

"You got this, brother. You can do it. We'll be out here if you need us." He kisses my cheek before pulling away.

I inhale deeply, filling my lungs with the warm air. I exhale slowly, then repeat the process a few more times, doing what I can to calm my nerves.

Rowen rubs my back soothingly, helping to calm me. Wiping my sweaty palms on my pants, I turn to face my childhood home and begin my journey across the street. The closer I get to the white door, the more my stomach aches with anxiety that threatens to cripple me.

Standing on the front step that my father once dragged me down on my last day here, I ball my hand into a fist and knock, breathing slowly through the memories that claw at the back of my mind.

The door swings open, and my eyes widen at the sight of the redhead woman in front of me.

Penny.

I've seen recent photos of her, and even if I hadn't, it's easy to tell who she is. She looks even more like her mother now that she's older.

"Can I help you?" she snarls, eyeing me from head to toe. Her eyes lock on mine, the wrinkles around her eyes becoming prominent as she squints. "A-A-Ace?" she gasps, her skin becoming pale. My eyes must've been how she recognized me because I know I don't look the same as I did. I'm no longer the scrawny boy she used to pick on.

Finding my voice, I open my mouth and speak. "Hello, Penny." My words come out calm despite how uneasy and shaken up I feel. "Is Father home?"

Crossing her arms, she steps out onto the porch, pulling the door halfway shut behind her. "What are you doing here?"

"I'm here to see my father. Is he home?"

"Why? You have no business being here," she snaps, her hands moving to her wide hips.

Taking a step closer to her, I look down my nose at her. "I want to see my father, and I will not ask again."

Before she can oblige, I hear the voice that's haunted my dreams for years.

"Who's at the door, sweetheart?" The door creaks open, and goosebumps line my flesh as I stand tall, coming face-to-face with my father for the first time since I was twelve.

His dark hair is dusted with grey, and wrinkles have taken over his face. I was once afraid of him, but staring at him now, I feel nothing.

My lip curls in disgust at the fact he stares at me without a single hint of recognition. "What's the matter; you don't recognize your oldest son?" My words are laced with the humor I suddenly feel, which is strange. But standing here in front of him, I can't help but feel the need to laugh. He looks like a normal loving family man, but I know that he's anything but. Abusers like him don't change. They are who they are, the sick scum of the earth.

My father blinks, glancing at his wife by his side before glancing back at me. "Ace?" A frown finds his lips. "Why don't you come inside, son?" He steps to the side, gesturing toward the front door.

"Son? That's funny. I remember you told me I was no longer your son and would never be welcome in your home or family again."

"That was a long time ago, Ace. You're obviously here for a reason, so what do you want?"

"To see you. That's all."

"What the fuck for?" Penny snaps, clicking her tongue.

Ignoring her, I look my father in his dark eyes that I once hated looking at because they reminded me of something evil. "You know, for years, I wondered what I did that was so wrong to cause you to hurt me the way you did. All those nights, you snuck into my bedroom and raped me, I thought it was my fault. I thought I deserved it. You said I was bad, and you were punishing me, but I know now that I did nothing wrong. There is nothing anyone could ever do, especially a child, that is so wrong that deserves that type of abuse. It was rape. That's what you did to me. You raped me for years! You never stopped no matter how much I cried and begged. You kept going until my asshole was a bloody mess." Years of built-up rage and anger flow through my veins, igniting my body on fire. The sick bastard has the audacity to look guilty and avert his gaze.

Not fucking today.

Stepping closer until we're toe-to-toe, I reach out and grip his jaw in my hand, forcing him to look me in the eye. "You. Raped. Me," I hiss, carefully pronouncing every single word.

Penny gasps. In my peripheral, I can see her lips moving but I'm unable to focus on whatever nonsense she's spewing.

"I spent too many fucking years wondering what I did to deserve your abuse and hoping that one day you'd find me and apologize. I loved you, and if you were to apologize, I would've forgiven you. Then one day, I realized you're scum. You're a pedophile. You are the worst type of person to exist. You chose your new family over me. Your own flesh and blood."

"What do you want me from me, Ace?" he grits out. "You want me to apologize?"

A slow grin spreads across my mouth. "No, I don't. I want nothing from you." Letting him go, I step away from him. "You're not worth anything. I have a family of my own, and I'm a better father than you ever were." I take another step away just as Penny comes running out of the house with a baseball bat in her hands, ready to swing.

"Get away from us!" she screams, shaking like a leaf while holding the bat. I could easily take it from her and use it to crush both of their skulls, but they're not worth it. I believe in karma, and it's going to get them both one day. I've paid for my sins in the years I spent away from my pretty thing. That was my karma.

They will get theirs. It's only a matter of time.

In the background, I hear King and Rowen rushing toward me at the sight of Penny holding the bat in front of me, my father hiding behind her life a fucking loser.

Her eyes widen at the sight of the two men behind me. "Get off our property!" she yells, her voice full of fear that used to get my dick hard. Nowadays, the only thing that gets my dick hard is my wife and the two guys behind me, who are ready to protect me.

"Who the fuck are they?" my father asks, finally choosing to man up by taking the bat from his wife.

"My family." I smile. "Goodbye, James." I choose to use his first name because I no longer feel anything for the man whom I share DNA with.

Turning, I walk to King and Rowen just as the front door slams shut. Penny and James wasted no time running inside. A chuckle leaves my lips at the sound of the deadbolt clicking.

"Are you okay?" King asks, worry in his hazel eyes.

"Did you get what you came for?" Rowen inquires.

Unable to keep the smile from my face, I give them an honest answer. "Yeah, actually. I am. And I got exactly what I came for."

I've been uncertain how I'd react to seeing James again. Even during the drive, I couldn't stop playing different scenarios in my head. It wasn't until I saw him face-to-face that I realized he's not the one I need to help me fully heal.

Saying what he did to me out loud released a major weight from my shoulders. I never realized that's what I needed to say until now.

Looking between King and Rowen, I wrap an arm around both of their shoulders, walking with them toward our car.

"What I need is both of you and our wife. Let's go home."

As Rowen drives away, I stare at the house in the mirror, feeling myself becoming more and more emotionally stronger the further we get from that house.

Everything I'll ever need to continue my healing journey is them.

My family.

The ones who truly love me and will never hurt me.

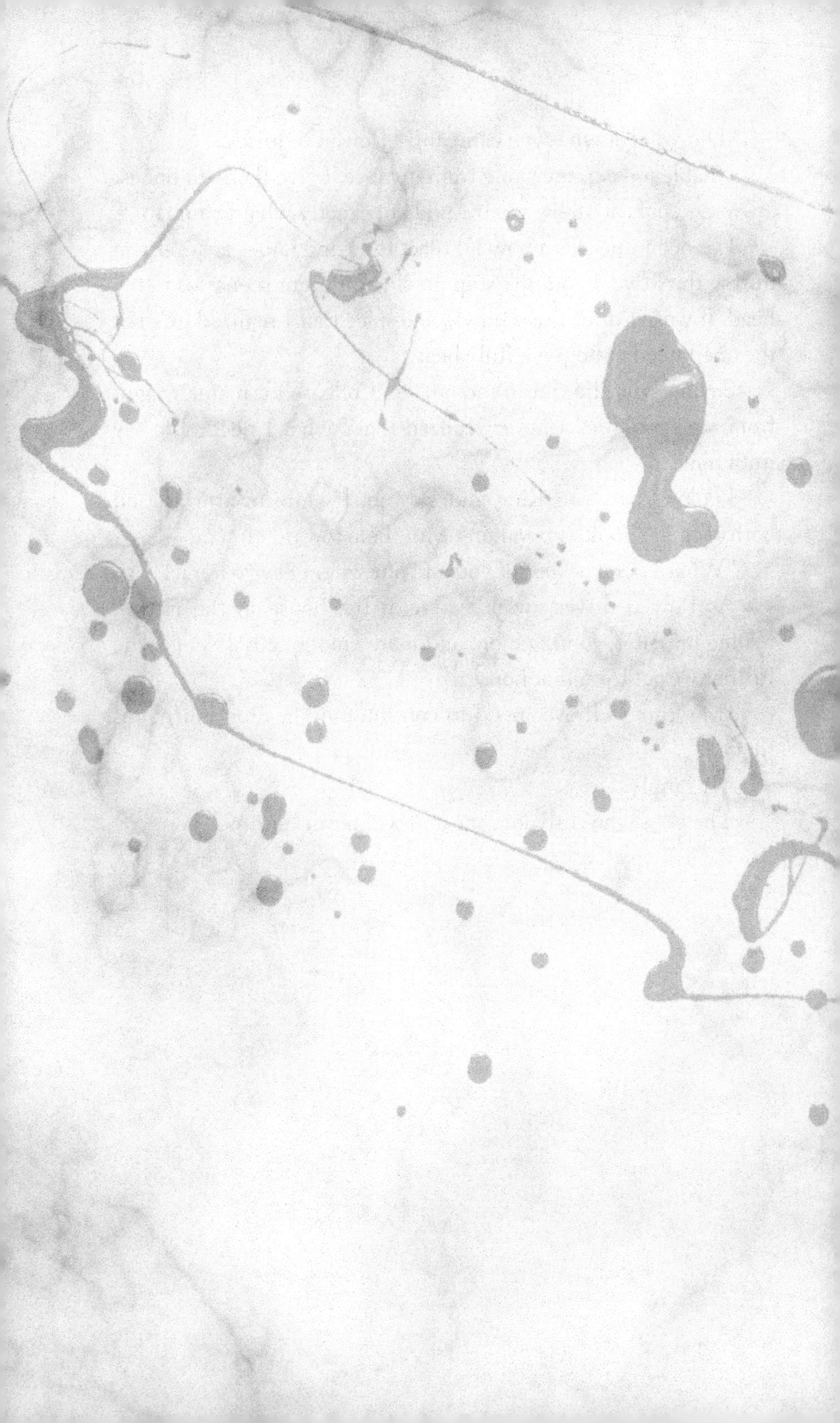

Chapter Fifteen

THIRTY-SEVEN YEARS OLD

PRESENT DAY

I ALWAYS KNEW THAT MY LIFE WOULD GET BETTER eventually. I knew that, one day, I'd have enough food in my fridge, a big-ass bed full of pillows, and someone to love me that would never abandon me.

No matter how many times life has kicked my ass and tried to keep me down, I knew that one day everything I've ever been through would all pay off. Through the years, I've had faith that everything would one day work out for me, and that my pretty thing would return to me.

Lee needed time to realize she belonged with me, and thank fuck she came to her senses. She certainly took her sweet time, but she was worth the wait.

Now, I have multiple people in my life that love me. I have a wife, partners, and children. The last two were completely fucking unexpected, but I'd never trade my family for anything.

All I've wanted since I was twelve was her. The girl with turquoise eyes who smiled and acknowledged me when everyone else ignored me. I'm one of the lucky bastards that gets to wake up beside her every single day, and sometimes, I still feel like I'm waiting for the other shoe to drop.

Some days my life feels like a dream, and I pray to God that I never wake up. I fear one day my inner demons will come to collect and drag me to hell—where I belong—for my sins. Every day I feel as if I'm living on borrowed time, and I haven't wasted a single second of it.

When you think about where I started compared to where I am now, it's unbelievable. I'm no longer that unwanted boy.

I'm wanted in so many ways, and every single day my wife shows me just how wanted I am.

I never thought I'd be okay with sharing my pretty thing long-term. Secretly, I'd been hoping that she'd realize she didn't need anyone else and would choose to be with me and only me. Instead of telling her how I felt, I kept it to myself because getting any piece of her was better than not having her at all. I was willing to share, knowing it would be temporary. We were never supposed to all be together long-term.

Then Eli died, and I realized I loved King and Rowen, too, and I didn't want to be without either of them. Call me fucking crazy, but after that night, I didn't have a problem sharing my pretty thing with two other men.

I don't know how the fuck she does it, but she gives us all equal attention. She keeps us all loved, fed, happy, and keeps our balls empty.

My pretty thing is fucking perfect.

I always knew that that twelve-year-old boy would get his

happy ending with that nine-year-old girl, and here we are. It's amazing what having a little hope can do.

Footsteps pull me away from my thoughts. Then, the sound I'll never get enough of makes my heart flutter.

"You're awake."

Looking from the ceiling to the source of the voice, a smile spreads across my face at the sight of my woman. She looks at me with those captivating eyes as a genuine smile spreads across her face. The girl who once rarely smiled is now never without a grin on her ethereal face. "Are you okay?"

"You're so beautiful. Come here, let me get a better look at you."

A blush tints her cheeks. She tries to hide her face by putting her head down, but I can still see her despite her shyness.

"No way, I'm a mess. I just got back from a run, and I'm sweaty and need to shower."

I adjust the pillow underneath my head, placing one hand behind my head and the other on my stomach. "A run? Really?" I raise an eyebrow, a grin on my lips.

"A jog," she says, bouncing back and forth on her sock covered feet. "Okay, fine, it was a fast walk." I knew it. My pretty thing doesn't run unless I'm chasing her.

"I have something for you."

"What is it?" Her eyes light up with excitement.

Smirking, I remove the blanket, revealing my naked body and hard cock that's standing at attention just for her.

Laughter erupts from her. "You're disgusting!" She kneels on the bed, and I don't waste a second grabbing her by the back of the neck, pulling her toward me, and crushing our lips together in a bruising, teeth-clattering kiss.

"You know something? I've loved you every single day since you were nine years old, but I love you the most today, at thirty-four."

"You know I love you, Ace. Where's this coming from?"

Shrugging, I lean up long enough to add another pillow underneath my head. "I've been thinking about my life a lot lately. About everything I've been through, and how despite it all, I survived and I'm right here with you. We're blessed, we have a great family, and it makes me emotional."

She climbs onto my lap and straddles me, but sits back on my thighs, ignoring my exposed cock.

"We're lucky, Ace."

"Baby, I've done some terrible shit. I shouldn't get a happy ending because of my sins, but somehow, here I am." My hands grip her thick thighs, pulling her closer toward me. She knows the sins I'm talking about, because I came clean and admitted to her I've killed more women than what she thought I had, and I've been doing it for longer than I allowed her to believe. Or course, she was angry. It took a while for her to forgive me, but she did, because that's the type of person she is.

"You deserve everything good in the world, my lover. Stop telling yourself that you don't." She leans forward, pressing a quick kiss to my lips. "I love you, forever."

"I know you do, baby." Gripping her legging-covered ass, I give it a squeeze. "But I want you to show me how much you love me."

"I need to shower," she protests but still climbs off my lap long enough to remove her skintight black leggings and socks, revealing the sweet bare pussy between her thick thighs. It doesn't matter that she's sweaty from exercise. That's never stopped me from eating her before, and she knows that. I prefer her a little dirty, anyway.

Her hands grip the white crop top, and she pulls it over her head, along with her sports bra. The clothing falls silently to the floor, her body bare before me, sweat glistening along her forehead and stomach.

She worked up a sweat from the heat, and I can't wait to feast on the buffet between her legs.

Removing the pillows from my head, I lie down flat. "Sit on my face."

"Ace, come on." She blushes, her white teeth sinking into her plump bottom lip as she debates the decision. Her eyes dart between the open bathroom door and me.

Smirking, I give her a subtle head shake. "I'm comfortable. Don't make me chase you. And if you keep talking, I'm going to fill your mouth with my cock and fuck your face."

"Fine!" she relents, climbing onto the bed. We both know she wants her pretty pussy eaten, but she's always so damn unsure of herself when it comes to me wanting her when she's dirty. She should know by now that none of us care if she's freshly showered or not. Nothing, absolutely nothing, could ever stop me from eating her sweet pussy.

A little sweat sure as fuck will not keep me away.

"Since you're keeping me waiting, I want you to suck my cock while you let me have my favorite meal."

"Oh, no, what a punishment." She smirks, her eyes darkening with lust at the mention of having me inside of her mouth.

My girl is a cock sucking pro. Half the time I'm worried she's trying to suck my soul from my head. Her mouth and lips were made to have a dick between them.

Lee climbs on top of me, settling her legs on either side of my head, and leans forward, her mouth swallowing my cock in one unexpected gulp.

"Shit." My cock jerks in her warm mouth. She pulls back, the flat of her tongue licking over the slit, collecting the bead of precum forming. If she's not careful, I'll blow my load in her mouth right now, like a teenage boy.

"Mmmm. You taste so good." She covers me again, her throat tightening around me when she swallows.

While she sucks my soul, I rub my nose against her hardened clit, inhaling her intoxicating scent, nearly getting dizzy from the delicious smell.

Gripping her peachy ass, my fingertips dig into the globes as I bring her closer to my mouth, my tongue sticking out and swiping over her core in one long lick, her body jerking on top of me.

Her moans vibrate against my shaft, making me jerk inside her mouth. Wetness drips from her core into my open mouth, burying my face in her perfect pussy. Pushing my fingers deep inside of her, I curl them upward to find her G-spot and massage the area that has her body shaking and her core flooding. She squeezes around me with a vise-like grip, holding my fingers so tightly that her pussy makes a squelching noise when I thrust them inside her repeatedly.

"Oh God, I'm going to come!" she yells, her back arching and mouth coming off my dick with a wet *pop*. "I'm going to come in your mouth, and you're going to lick me clean," she commands, her body shaking with the threat of an oncoming orgasm.

Continuing my work, I keep my fingers curled deep inside her and give the sensitive bud the attention it deserves, my lips sucking while my tongue circles the bud. By the way she's writhing and the way her pussy is pulsating, I know she's ready to come. I give her G-spot one more massage, then stop and pull my hand away when I feel the flood of fluid squirt from her.

She's always been an easy squirter. All it takes is the right touch.

"Fuck yeah, baby. Drown me." I open my mouth, drinking from her pussy like a fountain. My throat bobs as I swallow, her mouth wrapping around me once again.

Pushing my fingers back into her, her tight walls squeeze me and pulse around my fingers as I finger fuck her, coaching another orgasm from her body.

I remove my fingers and suck them clean, attacking her clit

once more with my mouth. This time, as her body shakes with her second orgasm, mine does, too.

My release is immediate, and like a good girl, she keeps sucking my head while I come, drinking every drop of cum I offer her. She milks me dry while giving me another fountain to drink from.

My pretty thing.

So fucking sweet.

Lee rolls on her back, her chest rising and falling rapidly as she fights for oxygen. "I'm too tired to shower now." She sighs, a content smile on her glistening face.

A click of the tongue has my head turning, making me look toward the noise. "Damn, seems like we should've come home sooner," Rowen says, a smirk on his lips from where he stands in the doorway.

"Fuck, that was hot." King groans beside him, my eyes landing on him just in time to catch him with his pants unbuttoned and dick is his hand, pumping over the hard length.

Lee laughs. "I'd get up to kiss you guys, but I'm too tired to move."

King pushes his pants down his legs, revealing the muscular thighs he's recently had tattooed. He has ink covering every inch of his skin, just like me, minus our faces. Stepping out of his discarded jeans, he walks toward the bed. "That's okay, butterfly. All you need to do is open up."

I watch from my now seated position as he stands at the edge of the bed, stroking himself over Lee's face, her mouth open and tongue sticking out to prepare for the warm salty meal she's about to receive.

Rowan joins us on the bed, his clothes discarded, cock hard and glistening with pre-cum.

"That's okay. If you're tired, I'll do all the work. Just stay on your back." I watch as Rowen climbs over her body, spreads her legs, and sinks inside of her heat, groaning at the feel of her pussy wrapped around him. His head hangs, and his body remains still for a moment before he grips her hips, sits back on his heels, and begins fucking her. Her heavy tits bounce with the movement, her little pink nipples pebbled and erect.

"Fuuuck, she feels incredible. Like heaven." He groans, his eyes closing to savor the feel.

Being inside of her is as close to heaven as sinners like us will ever get. Heaven is real, and it's between her legs.

Taking my dick in my hand, I stroke it while I watch Ro fuck our girl. Lee licks King's balls and underneath his shaft from her position on the bed.

"Open wide, butterfly. I'm about to feed you this dick," King groans. Two seconds later, his fist is tightening around his length and thick come shoots from his head, landing in streams on Lee's awaiting tongue, several drops missing and landing on her delicate throat and chest.

The sight is enough to make me reach my climax, my balls tightening and spine tingling at the sensation. Sitting up on my knees, I reach her bouncing body just in time to release myself on her chest, painting it white.

Rowen must enjoy seeing my cum mixed with King's on her skin, because he joins us, removing himself from her tight pussy just in time to shoot his load over her chest, his fluid mixing with ours.

I watch her heaving body, fascinated by the sight of our cum dripping down from her chest, trailing along her stomach, and landing in her belly button, filling the tiny hole.

Reaching a hand toward her, I dip a finger in the mess and trace it over her lips, licking my finger clean. "You look better when you wear our cum like lipstick."

King leans over her body, his pierced tongue darting out and dipping into her belly button, lapping up our combined fluid. He hums, his mouth closing around her as he sucks her clean. "Delicious." He smiles, flashing his pearly whites. His beard's damp and coated with cum.

"Let's shower," Rowen suggests, the first to climb off the bed. "Gotta get our girl nice and clean so we can get her dirty again."

Lee leans up on her elbows. "Fine. You can have me until it's time to pick the kids up from school." Years ago, that's not something I ever would've thought I'd hear her say.

King grabs her body, throwing her over his shoulder before heading to the bathroom.

Staring at my family, I smile as I realize my life is complete. Every single moment has led me here. I'm exactly where I'm meant to be, and all the pain was worth it to end up with these people, in this place.

This is where I'm meant to be.

THE END

Signed Copies

Do you want to own a signed copy of this book?

Order yours today:

www.kylafaye.com

Also by Kyla Faye

Down We Go Series:

Dollhouse (Book #1)

Ashes (Book #2)

Ace (Book #3)

Coming Soon! (Book #4)

Part Of Me Series:

Our Way Back (Book #1)

Coming Soon! (Book #2)

About the Author

Kyla Faye is a twenty-something author of dark, adult erotic, and contemporary romance. When she's not reading about romance, she's writing about it, trying to give a voice to the characters that live inside her head. She has a caffeine addiction and always has a candle burning.

You can find her on social media:

Instagram & TikTok: @authorkylafaye
Readers Group: Kyla's House Of Whores
Website: www.kylafaye.com

About the Author

[illegible]

You can find her on social media:

Instagram & TikTok: [illegible]

Facebook Group: [illegible]

Website: [illegible]

Acknowledgments

Phew! That is a wrap on a story that has been a long time coming! A HUGE shout out to my readers for being so damn patient with me. I know it took a very long time for Ace's story to come to light, and I hope I gave you the satisfaction you were looking for.

Thank you to my PAs Martha and Logan for sticking by me, supporting me, listening to my random babbles, being my cheerleaders and supporting me during this process. You are amazing, and I'm so grateful to have you guys!

My editors, Tori and Zee, thank you both for turning my trash into gold. You two are the fucking best.

Thank you to my street team, beta readers, arc readers, everyone, for loving Ace and being the best fucking hype team ever! This crazy writing and publishing process is SO much easier when you have such an incredible team to support you.

I'm serious when I say I wouldn't be able to do any of this without the support of my readers. We're a team, and I love you all so much.

XO,

KF

Made in the USA
Coppell, TX
29 April 2024

31838147R00095